THE TINDER-BOX

What could an international official in Nicaragua, a greedy Polish ex-cop in New York, an unscrupulous confectioner in Geneva, and a Cuban jailbird in Zurich possibly have in common? The answer is a shock to idealistic Galina Romanova, an interpreter for the United Nations. Her trendy Manhattan lifestyle seems a world away when she is sent to Geneva to cover the Reagan-Gorbachev summit and encounters a man who will stop at nothing in order to wield sinister influence at the United Nations . . .

NORTHUMBERLAND COUNTY

PAUL STANLEY

THE TINDER-BOX

Complete and Unabridged

LINFORD
Leicester

First published in Great Britain in 1989 by
Robert Hale Limited
London

First Linford Edition
published 2000
by arrangement with
Robert Hale Limited
London

British Library CIP Data

Stanley, Paul
    The tinder-box.—Large print ed.—
Linford mystery library
    1. Detective and mystery stories
    2. Large type books
    I. Title
    823.9'14 [F]

    ISBN 0–7089–5787–0

Published by
F. A. Thorpe (Publishing)
Anstey, Leicestershire

Set by Words & Graphics Ltd.
Anstey, Leicestershire
Printed and bound in Great Britain by
T. J. International Ltd., Padstow, Cornwall

This book is printed on acid-free paper

To my beloved family,
who made this book possible.

' . . . The evil that men do lives after them,
The good is oft interred with their bones.'

Julius Caesar, Shakespeare

Prologue

Managua, Nicaragua,
October 16th, 1986, 5 p.m.

Workmen were putting the finishing touches to the long ceremonial red carpet that stretched from the tarmac to the wooden dais erected a few hundred meters from the airport terminal. As far as the eye could see, there was a flurry of activity which even the relentless tropical heat and steam-bath humidity did not succeed in slowing down. Soldiers in khaki battle-gear were beginning to take up their positions on both sides of the carpet, forming two parallel lines which, to the casual observer, fell just short of being straight. This was, after all, Latin America, albeit with a deadly serious war on.

Except there were no casual observers at Managua airport on that particular day, for all regular flights had been

1

cancelled and passes were being thoroughly checked to make sure no unauthorized persons loitered in the area. Strict orders to ensure maximum security had come from President Daniel Ortega himself, for a great deal was at stake. Just a month before, in New York, President Ortega had laid his and his country's prestige on the line by inviting the Secretary General of the United Nations to visit Nicaragua. '*El proposito de esta visita,*' he had declared from the rostrum of the General Assembly, 'The purpose of your visit, Mr Secretary General, will be to see that the counter-revolutionary contra troops are indeed sowing devastation in our dear country, a country we are desperately trying to rebuild after years of Anastasio Somoza's corrupt rule. Come and see for yourself and tell the world what you have seen.' Leo Anders, recently elected Secretary General of the United Nations, had taken up President Ortega's challenge over the vehement protests of the American delegation and less than subtle threats from Washington. You can't please all Member States all the time, he reasoned, and he was certainly not going to be a pawn to super-power games, or a lackey at the service of any particular master, like some of his predecessors. He firmly believed in the ideal of the United Nations and in the independence of his high office. He had earned himself an international reputation as a brave and fair man who refused to take orders from anyone, even if they were called Reagan or Gorbachev.

The plane began its descent over Managua. Secretary General Anders sighed heavily, put out the twentieth of his sixty cigarettes and turned to his assistant.

'Brian, hand me the status report on Nicaragua, will you?' he said with the minimum of politeness. He despised the timid, self-serving bureaucrats who populated the Organization, nasty little men like Brian Crowley. Trouble was, reflected Leo Anders sadly, I am stuck with them because they are all on permanent contracts which mean life tenure. I wish I could fire all of this deadwood, beginning with Brian Crowley.

He felt someone tapping him on the

arm. Brian was flashing his English schoolboy smile, saying something.

'What?' barked the Secretary-General with unaccustomed rudeness.

Brian nearly jumped out of his seat. What have I done wrong, he thought desperately. Oh Jesus, the boss is mad at me. There goes my promotion . . . Somehow he found his voice.

'The file, sir, the file on Nicaragua,' he squeaked.

'Thank you, Brian, you've done a grand job.' The sarcasm went right over Brian Crowley's head. This is going to be a wonderful day, he thought.

It was Brian Crowley's last thought in this life. Neither he, nor Secretary General Anders, nor any of the dozen senior officials on the plane had time to panic when they heard the deafening explosion that ripped the fuselage apart like a sheet of paper.

There was the briefest instant of pain as fire roared into the cabin, then nothing.

Debris fell out of the hazy sky like a shower of meteorites.

Washington, D.C.,
October 16th, 1986, 6 p.m.

A chilly autumnal night fell over the Capital, a Friday night of parties and secret trysts, political and amorous. Throughout the seat of the Federal Government, lights were being switched off in monolithic office buildings, and on in graceful town houses where the rich and the powerful played their weekend turf.

Only one house on a quiet street in the wealthy residential area of Georgetown remained dark. Officially, the Senator who owned it was away for the weekend which was not at all unusual for members of Congress who were frequently out of town, keeping in touch with their constituencies back home. Or so the accepted version went.

It was cold inside the house, downright chilly, in fact, he reflected, rubbing his well-manicured hands together vigorously.

If only that phone call would come. Lighting a cigarette, yet another, for he

5

had lost count of the coffin nails he had smoked in one short evening, he glanced at the luminous dial of his watch. Taking the time difference into account, in Managua it would now be . . .

The phone rang. He could not believe it, but it did. On the third ring, he picked up. There was crackling on the line, the sound was so faint it seemed to be coming from underwater, but the voice was familiar.

'*Patria o muerte. Venceremos,*' the caller said.

'Well done, Phoenix. No survivors?'

'None.'

'You can collect, then.'

'*Gracias, amigo.*' There was a click and the phone went dead. For a brief moment, his jubilant mood made him forget all common sense. He stood up, whistling softly to himself. The tune was 'God Bless America', and he felt like breaking out into full-throated song, but his sense of self-preservation won out and he quietly made for the front door.

A few minutes later, he was safely on his way to Dulles Domestic Airport, where he would catch the first shuttle to New York City. So much had happened, he reflected, so much in so short a time. It was, after all, barely a year ago that he had become involved in a series of extraordinary events that had brought him so close to success, so very close to the top . . .

1

New York, November 1985

Galina shivered, pointlessly huddling against the icy blast of wind billowing from the East River in relentless gusts. It was a bitter November Monday of leaden skies and Arctic temperatures, one of those Mondays that should never have happened in the first place, she thought grimly. Bracing herself against recurring polar blasts, she exchanged a brief nod with the unfortunate guard whose fate it would be to man the gate all morning, and walked towards the great revolving doors that marked the entrance to the United Nations Secretariat building. Behind her, the wind tore at the flags of one hundred and sixty three Member States so angrily that it threatened to wrench them from their ropes and send them floating all over Manhattan. And why not, thought Galina wryly; maybe the

9

Organization would then be better off.

With some difficulty, she pushed the heavy door open by leaning her whole slight frame against it. There was a time, she reflected, when the mere sight of United Nations Headquarters evoked distant dreams of gloss and glamour, unattainable visions of politics and power played on a world scale. There was a time, nearer to this day, when she had first walked into the matchbox-shaped house of glass and lies and had fancied herself right at the nerve centre of international decision-making. And finally, there had been a time, still nearer to this bleak Monday, when she had first sat in the English booth high atop the General Assembly building and tried to make sense of statements she heard in Russian, French or Spanish and, while putting them into English, wondered what the hell it was all about.

Warm, dry air wrapped her like an eiderdown as she walked through the lobby and down to the Interpretation Service offices in the basement. Glancing at her watch, she realized it was nearly ten thirty and she would probably be late for her meeting. Although she knew full well that delegates never assembled on time, etiquette demanded that Secretariat staff, including interpreters, man their posts at the appointed hour.

Galina stepped up her pace, tottering somewhat uncomfortably on the seven-inch heels she insisted on wearing to add a measure of stature to her five feet two inches. She dashed into the doorway, tearing off her soggy raincoat, and stopped in her tracks. The office was nearly empty, as most of her colleagues were by now in their respective booths or in the cafeteria, but the tiny cluster of those still checking their mail all looked up and stared at her. So did the two secretaries, Donna and Maud. It was as if Galina had truly made an entrance. Of all times, on a wet Monday morning.

'Hi,' she muttered, a bit irritated. 'I know I'm late and soaked and not your idea of a movie queen right now, but what's up? Why are you all staring at me as if someone had just told you I've developed an overnight case of AIDS?'

'Boss wants to see you.' Ageless, efficient Donna was solemn. Maud, heavily made up and impeccably dumb, just flashed a smile for all seasons.

'You mean Heller?' Galina winced. The mere sight of obese, servile Ronald Heller, the Chief Interpreter who had reached his post by licking every highly placed posterior in the United Nations, was an obscenity.

'No, higher than that.'

'Donna, I've never liked guessing-games. Suppose you just tell me.'

Donna's hint of a smile vanished altogether. She hated being put down, especially by interpreters, who in the view of the nine-to-five girl that she was doomed to be, were a bunch of overpaid lazy bastards. True, Galina thought, my salary is twice Donna's, and for a twenty-one-hour week. Suddenly, she felt rich and glamorous and compassionate.

'Sorry, Donna, Monday-morning blues.' Her tone and face were much softer now.

'It's all right, I'm used to you people being temperamental.' So she is not going to forgive me after all, thought Galina. Never mind. 'It's the big boss wants to see you,' continued Donna, awe creeping into her voice, 'the SG.'

'Anders?' gasped Galina in utter disbelief. 'What could he possibly want with me?'

'How should I know? He said to send you up the minute you come into the office. I have already made arrangements for Joe to replace you on the Security Council this morning.'

'Great. I can't say I'm sorry to miss another fruitless debate on the Iran — Iraq war.'

'No comment. Will you please go up to the thirty-eighth floor right now? The Secretary-General is expecting you.'

'Right.' As she turned to leave, she caught a passing glimpse of herself in the glass partition wisely erected to separate Donna from Maud. I look a mess, she thought, pointlessly trying to smooth a tangled mop of shoulder-length streaked hair that stood out in all sorts of interesting directions. I can't possibly go and meet the Pontifex Maximus looking like a punk. At my age, too. As far as she was concerned, being thirty-five was way over the hill.

*   *   *

As soon as Galina was ushered into the Secretary General's vast, sparsely furnished office, she realized she need not have been so apprehensive about her appearance after all. Rumour had it that Leo Anders was a man concerned far more with substance than with looks, and rumour was, for once, spot on. Galina found herself instantly taking to the gentle, intelligent brown eyes that regarded her with humour from under an abundant head of silvery hair. He was wearing an old tweed jacket and smoking a pipe, every inch the university professor he had once been.

'Good morning, Miss Romanova,' he said pleasantly, a trace of his native Dutch accent obvious in his otherwise excellent English. 'I'm so sorry to inconvenience you so early on a Monday morning, but this is important. Please take a seat,' he continued, indicating a soft beige leather armchair across from the wide expanse of his mahogany desk.

'I'm sure you know Nikolai Golovin.' The other occupant of the room, seated directly across from the Secretary General, sprang to his feet.

So this is Nikolai Golovin, the Soviet star interpreter whose name seems to be on everybody's lips these days. Unlike his lesser colleagues, he did not come to the United Nations on a five-year tour of duty. From what Galina had heard, he appeared in Western Europe or the United States only when a major conference or a meeting between top officials was taking place. He looks important, she thought, important and self-confident. And stylish. His tan suit was impeccably cut, calculated just right enough to play down a certain heaviness of frame which would have made him look squat had he not been tall. He was as dark as she was fair. He looked, in fact, Georgian, with his aquiline nose and olive skin, although the surname, she knew, had nothing Georgian about it.

They shook hands. '*Ochen pryatno*,' she said. 'Very pleased to meet you.'

His thick eyebrows went up. 'Do you speak Russian, then?' he answered in flawless mid-Atlantic English. 'How come?'

'I interpret from Russian, Mr Golovin.'

'So what? That still doesn't mean you are fluent in it.'

'All right. My parents were Russian.' He knows, she thought, everyone knows everything about everyone else in this milieu. The Soviets, the Americans, they all play the same silly James Bond game.

'I'm really glad you seem to have hit it off', Leo Anders intervened. 'Because you see, Miss Romanova, you are going to be teamed up very shortly. Mr Golovin, who has just arrived from Washington where he has been covering a series of pre-summit meetings between Secretary Schultz and Ambassador Dobrynin, is going to be your travelling companion on a trip to Geneva. The two of you are going to be the back-up team at the Reagan — Gorbachev meeting.'

'You look shell-shocked.' Nikolai

smiled at her a trifle condescendingly, which infuriated her.

Indeed I do, she thought. Why me, when I'm not even senior enough to land such a plum assignment. My colleagues are going to love me for this. Whatever the reason, I must look as if I can handle it.

She studied Nikolai Golovin coolly. 'Maybe you are used to this high-flying type of work, Mr Golovin . . . '

'Nikolai Sergeevich.'

'Nikolai Sergeevich.' What a miracle he didn't ask me to call him him tovarisch. Maybe before we get through this we'll really be comrades, she thought wryly. Or at least he'll try hard to turn me into one.

The Secretary-General's soft voice burrowed into her thoughts. 'Make sure you get all the paperwork done right away. I'm signing your travel authorizations myself. You leave for Geneva tomorrow.'

★   ★   ★

'How long are you going to be gone?' Bill sounded unusually forlorn. But then, he had been an unusually ardent lover this evening. They were lying on the large circular double bed in his Waterside Plaza condominium, sipping champagne. Bill could not abide vodka, Galina's favourite drink. Far below them, the lights of New York danced on the East River.

'A week, maybe ten days, maybe longer. I might take a little holiday in Europe after the summit.'

'May I join you?'

She stared at him wide-eyed. This was not like him at all. In the five years they had been together, she had known him to take three days off at the very outside, and by the third morning he was usually in an impossible mood, raring to get back to the city and to his office, imagining all sorts of disasters that had befallen the company in his absence. And now he wanted to take a holiday with her, a real holiday away from his beloved stocks and shares. Incredible.

'Why, that's wonderful, Bill. I thought the day would never dawn when you'd want to take an actual trip with me. And not just to the Hamptons, but to Europe. Wow.'

'I'll miss you, my darling,' he whispered, burying his face in her hair.

'So will I, sweetheart, so will I,' she answered absently, wondering why she could not dismiss the uncomfortable feeling that had been with her since she left the Secretary-General's office a few hours earlier. More than an actual feeling, it was a vague sense of disquiet that tugged at the back of her mind, a sensation that her trip to Geneva would change something and change it forever in her life. Lying there, in Bill's arms, she suddenly did not want to leave him, because it meant leaving home. Nonsense, she told herself, you can't back out of the assignment now, or else Anders will quite rightly think you are totally nuts. It's only Geneva, after all, not Timbuctoo, and what could be more glamorous than being involved in a historic summit meeting between the leaders of the two superpowers?

Then why, she thought with annoyance, why this hunch that once I step into the plane, there will be no going back?

2

Swissair flight 101 from New York touched down at Geneva airport at precisely ten past seven in the morning, according to Captain Knoepfli's infallible Omega watch. Over the intercom, the captain's proud voice crackled, 'Leities und shentlemen, ve khev shust lendet at Cointrin Airport, Sheneve, tventy minutes ahet of schedule.' Twenty minutes. Unbelievable, thought Galina, putting her book away in her flight-bag. She had heard about the legendary precision of the Swiss, but this was an aberration, punctuality run amok. She took out her make-up kit, produced her compact and examined her bleary face. She had tried to minimize the devastating effects of a transatlantic trip by wearing little make-up, refraining from drink and sitting in the non-smoking section, tips she had

21

picked up from a host of magazines for the high-powered professional woman who always looked her best.

The non-smoking section, moreover, had seemed a perfect idea when Nikolai Golovin, whom she had spotted ahead of her on the check-in line at Kennedy, along with several people from the Soviet mission to the United Nations, asked for a seat in the smokers. At all costs, she would try and avoid him as long as she could, or at least have little to do with him, because she sensed his charm could, given free play, turn into a fairly lethal weapon. Never trust the Soviets, her mother had said, they will always do their best to win you over for their purposes. Her mother, whose parents had left Russia fleeing from the 1917 Revolution, had never met any Soviets, which did not prevent her from having very definite ideas about them. Her father, also a Russian refugee, was far less definite because, to him, the world was a formidable twine of complicated motives you could not reduce to the mere basics of good and evil. Still, Papa, politics is politics, thought Galina, addressing her father across the five years he had been dead. She tried not to think about her parents, but the pain came unbidden. They had died still young, in their sixties and within six months of each other, leaving Galina totally bereft of family. With them, they had taken her love and whatever little she knew about her Russian heritage and, in exchange, left her a set of moral principles, a superb education and the language of her ancestors, which she had learned to use very well. That language had become her only home, a mythical place of worship and rest from a world in which she was perpetually an alien. That language also happened to be Nikolai Golovin's mother tongue, making her particularly sensitive and vulnerable to their common roots.

The plane taxied to a stop in front of a satellite terminal and the passengers patiently filed out under low grey skies that spewed a merciless icy sleet on them.

'Mind you don't slip. It's a skating rink out here.' Out of the corner of her eye, Galina saw Nilokai's dark profile bending solicitously towards her. 'May I?' And without waiting for an answer, he gripped her arm tightly and steered her towards the entrance.

'Depressing weather,' he commented, ignoring the mixture of surprise and annoyance in Galina's eyes. 'November in Geneva is hopelessly grim.'

'Have you been here before, then?'

'Frequently.' His smile held humour and mystery at the same time.

'You must know the place pretty well then.'

'There isn't much to know. It's not as exciting as New York or London or Paris. In fact, it's a dead bore.'

'You seem to travel a lot.'

It was a few seconds before he answered, fussing with the door, opening it for Galina.

'*Mnogo, da.* Too much,' he said when they were inside the terminal. I wonder what the neutral tone hides, thought Galina.

'Let's see how long it takes us to get through passport control. Anywhere between two and five minutes, depending on the length of the line. As there is nothing the Swiss don't know . . . '

'Is there anything you don't know?' She wished she hadn't sounded quite so nasty.

He looked at her coolly. 'Oh yes.'

'For instance?'

'There's a great deal about you I don't know.'

'Haven't your people filled you in?'

'Have yours filled you in about me? What do you think, Galina? That the world is some kind of screwy place where Soviets and Americans chase each other with bugs and poisoned darts? Wake up, my dear Miss Romanova. Times have changed, in your country and in mine. This is why our two leaders are meeting.'

'I wish I could believe that.'

'Then do. The more we put into changing our mentality, the more of a chance we stand of saving this planet. That is what it's all about.'

'Do you always have such serious discussions at seven o'clock in the morning?' she asked wearily.

'Only when I think I have a worthwhile partner to discuss with.'

For the briefest of moments, their eyes locked and held.

Nikolai had been absolutely right about the speed and efficiency of Swiss authorities. The immigration official took Galina's passport, eyed it with seeming indifference, handed it back and waved her through. Amazingly enough, he performed the same pantomime with Nikolai. He must be either very highly placed or valuable to the Swiss to get through so easily on a Soviet passport, concluded Galina. Intriguing, very intriguing, this Nikolai Sergeevich Golovin. Well, it was none of her business anyhow. She would complete her assignment — which, she had to admit, was one of the most exciting to come any interpreter's way — do a bit of travelling in Europe and go home. She probably would not be seeing that much of Nikolai anyway, except at working sessions and official functions.

She was dead wrong!

★   ★   ★

26

Basil Crimer was known around the State Department as a cocky bastard. Born Vasily Krymov to Russian emigrés who had settled in Boston, where his father had landed a Russian History chair at Harvard, young Vasily made it through the prestigious university on full scholarship. As he grew up, blue-eyed and handsome on the playing fields of Harvard, he knew he had been exceptionally lucky for a foreigner with no connections to that patrician Ivy League stronghold. When he graduated *summa cum laude*, he consolidated his luck by marrying La Donnia Granville-Parker, a Radcliffe heiress with a sexual appetite as sizable as her fortune, both outrageously large by New England standards. La Donnia, who prided herself on being one of the pillars of the *Mayflower* set, could not possibly go through life calling herself Mrs Krymov. Accordingly, not long after the wedding, Vasily Krymov became Basil Crimer. At least, he reasoned, he had got something out of the marriage — an American-sounding name and a sizeable settlement when La Donnia left him.

Although she blamed him for his many affairs, she never stopped loving him, worse, desiring him, and he knew it. In exchange for his promise to sleep with her even after the divorce, she contracted to pay him a handsome monthly sum. Though he was heartily sick of her stupidity and her fulsome blondness, the money was compensation enough for his pains. Being a gigolo had never bothered him.

Armed with his new American sounding name and his old Russian charm, Basil Crimer moved to Washington and went to work for the State Department as an interpreter. He really wanted to become a career diplomat, but he thought he would make himself indispensable by the excellence of his Russian, especially in bilateral Soviet — American talks. At first, he thought his job would be a stepping stone to bigger and better things, but diplomacy was a field where his obvious foreignness was a decided hindrance. That was in the sixties, long before it became fashionable to be Russian, long before a foreigner succeeded in becoming

American Secretary of State. Basil Crimer never forgave that foreigner, whose name happened to be Henry Kissinger, and with whom he frequently travelled to the Soviet Union as official interpreter. Nor did he find it easy to forgive fellow United States citizens who looked down on him as a hyphenated American, for he was a patriot among patriots, whose virulent hatred of the Soviet regime made Senator Eugene McCarthy seem an open-minded liberal.

On that particular November morning at the American mission in Geneva, Basil Crimer was pacing up and down the rectangular conference-room where the first working-session of the Reagan — Gorbachev summit was to be held. He was impeccably turned out in a grey pin-striped suit and beige tie, and he stood tall and proud and lithe despite his fifty-two years. But his mood was black and he was impervious to the cheery face of his raven-haired actor president who smiled benignly at him from a large photograph on the wall.

'What the hell do the idiots in

Washington and New York think they are doing?' he nearly screamed at Tony Biddle, the young Protocol Officer at the American mission. 'Sending me some sort of vaguely qualified girl to a high-level meeting. Isn't it enough I have to put up with all those Soviets milling about? Gorbachev's a sham, I tell you, Tony, with all his openness and recon-struction and high-sounding empty rhetoric. Just propaganda,' he snorted with contempt, 'to take in decent Americans like you and me. I really don't know what our President is doing, meeting with that hypocrite who wants to conquer the world for Communism.'

Our President, thought Tony. He is not your President, you pretentious Russki bastard. Aloud he said, 'I hear Miss Romanova's very good.'

'I'll bet you a hundred dollars she'll fall flat on her face in the first five minutes.'

They shook hands. When Crimer wasn't looking, Tony Biddle hastily wiped the palm that had made contact with the Russian-American.

★　　★　　★

A uniformed bell-hop showed Galina to
her room at the Hotel Beau Rivage, one
of the most elegant establishments in a
land renowned for its tradition of
excellent hotel service. It was a large
bedroom entirely upholstered in delicate
cream wallpaper. The bedspread matched
the heavy silk peach drapes, open to
reveal a very wintry view of Lac Leman.
She walked to the bedside table, turned
on the radio and Mozart's sublime music
inundated the room, filling her with
peace. For a brief painful moment, she
wished she could pick up the phone and
call her mother in New York and describe
all this wonderful luxury to her. Over the
years, she had been in the habit of calling
her parents from wherever she happened
to be, of sharing her adventures with
them, for they lived a strange isolated life.
After a lifetime of different languages and
countries and continents, they were too
exhausted to make new friends, to meet
new people. So they had turned in upon
each other and upon her, their only child,

31

their consolation after an eternity of poverty and rootlessness. It had been a heavy burden on her, but she had loved them dearly enough to give up her own free time to spend it with them in their small apartment on Manhattan's unfashionable West Side. Her life of luxury and travel was in striking contrast to their own dull routine of work and television, and they were glad for her. Now, the memory of their incredible goodness was a lump in her throat.

Galina had been so absorbed in her memories that she had failed to notice the enormous bouquet of long-stemmed red roses on the dressing-table. Who could possibly be sending me flowers here, she thought, it must be a mistake. Cautiously, she picked up the attached card and took it out of its small envelope. It read, in Cyrillic script so beautifully cursive it seemed to slither off the paper, 'What an interesting coincidence that we are at the same hotel. Maybe we could get together some time and drink to our enduring partnership. Nikolai Golovin.'

Never in a million years, she thought angrily.

★ ★ ★

Two floors up from Galina, Nikolai picked up the phone. 'I would like to place an urgent call to Moscow,' he told the operator in barely accented French.

'*Bien sûr, Monsieur Golovine. Tout de suite.*'

Nikolai walked to the small well-stocked bar, poured himself a Black Label Scotch, lit a Dunhill and settled down for the brief wait. His call would go through in a few minutes, and he would have some explaining to do. But it did not worry him, not as long as he was safely out of the country.

3

Natalia Golovin was in a state of barely-controlled fury. She could have torn her husband Nikolai to pieces, clawed his eyes out with her long perfect nails. Ever since his call from Geneva an hour before, her anger had been rising like a fever inside her. The sound of the phone had wrenched her out of her much-needed sleep, after a gruelling day in her new job as Director of the Culture Commission. She loved her work, but it was extremely demanding and she felt under constant pressure to do her best as co-ordinator of the new flourishing exchange programme with the West in the performing-arts field. Nikolai should have known better than to disturb her at nearly midnight. After all, his own career was everything to him, so why could he not respect hers? Typical Soviet male chauvinist, she snorted with contempt, no matter how highly placed, no matter how sophisticated, he always imagines he comes first in the overall scheme of things, to the absolute exclusion of everybody else. As if she were a mere housewife, instead of a former prima ballerina at the Bolshoi, equal to Ulanova and Plesetskaya, and like them an Artist of the Soviet Union. For all Nikolai cared, she could have been an ordinary peasant. *Svoloch*, she swore under her breath, *kakaya svoloch*. What a creep.

'*Natasha, ia v Zheneve*,' he had calmly announced when she picked up the phone.

It had taken a few seconds for the news to sink in through her thick veil of sleep. '*Gde?*' she asked incredulously when she gathered her wits. 'Where?' she repeated, her voice rising to a shrill pitch.

'In Geneva. I'm doing the Reagan — Gorbachev summit.'

'What?' exploded Natalia. 'This is the giddy limit, Nikolai. First you're off to Washington for a few days and you refuse to take me along on the pretext that I've been there and it's not worth it for such a short trip, and next thing I know you call me up at midnight to tell me you're doing the summit. You know how much I would have enjoyed that, how little opportunity I have to get out of Moscow. Are you ashamed of me then? Or are you running another one of your convenient little affairs, Nikolai?' She heard herself yelling and she knew she sounded like a fishwife, but somehow she could not stop.

'Calm down, Natasha, please . . . '

'Calm down? You treat me like a discarded old rag, and you want me to calm down. You've got a nerve, Nikolai, you really do . . . '

'Natasha.' The more heated she got, the calmer he sounded, and he knew that always infuriated her. 'Natasha, *slushai*. Listen to me, please. You know we are both very busy, we've got very demanding jobs . . . '

'Is that why you call me up in the middle of the night?'

' . . . and you also remember you couldn't have come in any case, you are

36

far too busy with the Culture Commission . . . '

'Yes, I remember. But then I didn't
know you were going on to Geneva. If I
had, I could have taken some time off,
had a much-needed holiday. But you
don't care, do you Nikolai, you don't give
a damn about my work or my health — or
me, for that matter. Why pretend?'

She heard him sigh heavily. Obviously,
he was not going to bother contradicting
her. They both knew that, for years now,
theirs was an empty marriage, a sham
they both kept up because divorce would
have ruined their careers and that was
more than either of them could stand.

'Is there anything I can bring you?' he
asked lamely.

Natalia slammed the phone down.

She reached over to the bedside table
and picked up her cigarettes with a
violently shaking hand. She lit one,
inhaled deeply and looked around the
room as if trying to draw strength from
the success it symbolized. They were all
there, the trappings of the Soviet
Nomenklatura; the Italian furniture, the

English drapes, the Moravian crystal vases. She well remembered how they had moved into this apartment on Herzen Street, in one of the oldest, most exclusive neighbourhoods in Moscow. Everything had seemed bright and promising and joyful then, with Nikolai graduating brilliantly from the prestigious Institute for Foreign Languages, while she, Natalia, had landed her first major role as prima ballerina of the Bolshoi. Their lifestyle was a mirror of a success totally inaccessible to the vast majority of their Soviet comrades. But the lot of the masses meant little to the Golovins. They had not made the Revolution — they just reaped its benefits. Over the years, they had revelled in the glamour and prestige accorded only to Party members, living the gilded life of the elite, spending a good deal of their time abroad, furnishing their splendid home with endless mementos of their foreign travels, amassing a small fortune while, almost imperceptibly, their love faded.

Natalia stubbed out her cigarette. Suddenly she felt old, beached like a hollow shell. Hollow and angry. *Svoloch*, she thought, bastard. You don't get rid of me so easily. You'll pay me back all right, you'll pay me back a thousandfold, Nikolai Golovin. First thing in the morning, she decided, she was going to see her old friend Arkady Rudenko.

★   ★   ★

Colonel Arkady Petrovich Rudenko, Deputy Chief of the KGB, had his own problems, not the least of which was a splitting headache. He had been under intolerable pressure lately, and his health was beginning to suffer, which largely accounted for his foul mood on that bleak November morning. He sat brooding behind his massive desk at *KGB* Head-quarters, Two Dzerzhinsky Square, an address bitterly known to dissidents the length and breadth of the Soviet Union. Colonel Rudenko had inherited the desk and the office from his predecessor, Gennadi Lopukhov, who had taken over as Chief when Yuri Andropov had been singled out for bigger and better things as undisputed master of the Kremlin. But, reflected Rudenko grimly, when Andropov was boss of the KGB, the venerable institution's very name was synonymous with power and prestige. Not any more, not since Gorbachev had set in motion his openness and res-tructuring and Western-style liberalism. *Yerunda*, he concluded, rubbish, absolute rubbish. Oh, for the glorious days of Stalin, when the mere mention of the NKVD, the dreaded *Narodni Komissariat Vnutrennikh Del*, was enough to strike fear in the most loyal comrade's heart.

There was a sharp knock on the door, wrenching Rudenko out of his sweet memories and transporting him back to the unpalatable present.

'*Da*,' he barked.

A young man with broad, flat features entered timidly and stood shuffling from foot to foot. Rudenko looked up, his eyes questioning. 'Comrade Colonel,' the youth began, 'Com-com-com-rade Colonel . . . '

'What is it, Kostya?' asked Rudenko gruffly. 'Out with it. I'm a busy man, I don't have all day.'

'Comrade Natalya Golovina to see you.'

'What?'

'Comrade Golovina to see you, Comrade Colonel. She is . . . '

'I know who she is, you fool. Did she have an appointment?'

'I don't believe so.'

Although he appeared to hesitate for his underling's benefit, Rudenko knew full well he could not possibly turn Natalia away. She was, after all, Raisa Gorbacheva's personal protegée, appointed by the First Lady herself to head the Culture Commission, a seemingly innocuous honorary post that in actual fact was one of the most powerful in the Soviet Union. He had known Natalia far too long, had once been far too close to her to forget how vindictive she could be if she only chose. To cross her would entail too many risks and Rudenko had always hated the unpredictable.

★   ★   ★

There she stood now, regal in her ankle-length sable coat, her green eyes gleaming dangerously. She was far more beautiful than he remembered her, than she had been as a young girl, he thought admiringly.

'*Dobry den*, Natasha,' he began more softly than he had intended.

She cut him off sharply. 'There is nothing good about this morning, Arkady. I want you to do me a favour, for old times' sake.'

'Is it a request or an order?' he asked half in jest. Natasha's requests, he knew all too well, were always orders.

'Don't make light of it, Arkady.'

'What's your pleasure, *tovarisch*?' He was unable to keep the bitterness out of his voice.

'I'm sure you are aware that my husband Nikolai is in Geneva for the summit.'

Rudenko nodded. Was he just! Nikolai Golovin, as far as he was concerned, had too much freedom. As one of Gorbachev's darlings, he travelled wherever he pleased whenever he pleased, totally bypassing the KGB. The worst of it was, there was nothing in the world Rudenko, or even his boss, could do without setting themselves on a direct collision course with the General Secretary himself.

'Well, I want him followed.'

'But . . . '

'No buts, Arkady. I want your men on his tracks. I know Nikolai. Sooner or later he will get himself into some kind of trouble, presumably with a woman, and I want your boys to be there and catch him red-handed. Am I making myself clear?'

The Chief of the KGB swallowed hard. 'Couldn't be clearer.'

'Can I count on you then?' Natalia's lips curled into a smile that was more like a grimace.

'Have I ever let you down?'

'*Dosvidanya*, Arkady.' And, before he knew it, she was gone.

Rudenko buried his head in his hands helplessly. This was not going to be easy. If Gorbachev ever found out that one of his favourites was being interfered with, the Deputy Chief of the KGB could kiss all his perks goodbye. One false move, and he would find himself enjoying early retirement in Central Asia.

He pressed the intercom button. 'Dimitry Pavlovich,' he barked when his assistant came on the line, 'I want to see you in my office, on the double. Drop everything you are doing. It's very urgent.'

* * *

Nikolai watched the watery morning light filtering through the half-open curtains in his room at the Beau Rivage, and hopelessly wished the day away. He had slept fitfully, which was unusual for him, and awakened early with the unpleasant sensation that he had done something irreparably stupid. He strained to remember what it was, and it was not long before the argument with his wife surfaced like an acrid taste in his mouth.

Calling Natalia, he realized now, had been a damn fool move. Why he had done it, he still failed to grasp entirely. Guilt, perhaps, or some vague and pointless desire to patch up a relationship that could never in the world be repaired. They were too far gone, he and Natalia, and there were times when he thought their disastrous marriage hurt him infinitely more than it hurt her.

He lit one of his Dunhill cigarettes, though he knew all too well he should not be smoking before breakfast, and stretched lazily, his thoughts drawn to Natalia as if he had not the will to channel them in any other direction. Their marriage had not always been disastrous, far from it. Twenty years ago, he remembered, when he first saw her darting across the stage of the Bolshoi in the scarlet costume of Stravinsky's *Firebird*, her long graceful arms fluttering like wings, he was irremediably smitten. Nikolai had always suspected himself of being a romantic, but he had not realized that his wild Russian soul would want to lay the world at his ballerina's feet.

He and Natalia had both been twenty-five then, and as madly in love with each other as two people can be. Or at least he was. For soon after their marriage, Nikolai discovered that his

45

young wife had very little time for love, or for anyone other than herself and her career. Nikolai supposed that, had he been less successful, she would have left him without any qualms. But he was, in fact, one of the brightest stars in the Soviet diplomatic constellation, and his excellent knowledge of English and of the West turned him into one of the top Foreign Ministry interpreters and, later, into a trusted advisor to Foreign Minister Shevardnadze.

Even if he and Natalia were no longer lovers, he reflected, they could still be glamorous allies and partners, presenting a successful, polished image of the new Soviet elite to the world. He was certain that, deep down, she felt the same way. She was sore because she had been left out and, in a sense, he could understand her, although whenever he was away from her, he felt a free man. Which reminded him of Galina Romanova. She seemed sweet and pretty and, despite her cold manner, strangely vulnerable to his charm.

He would try and have a drink with

her, perhaps more. And if that beautiful bitch Natalia took it into her head to get difficult, he could always pull out the insidious little secret that was his trump card, a secret that could destroy her in a matter of hours.

He knew that would be a last resort he would deeply regret.

4

Geneva, November 1985

Galina's first impression of Basil Crimer was that he spelled trouble. She seldom ignored or went back on first impressions and, if she did, it was almost invariably with disastrous results. Almost directly on meeting him, at the pre-summit staff briefing in the United States mission, she had felt uncannily apprehensive. His subsequent behaviour bore her feelings out.

To begin with, when she was introduced to Crimer, she had thought it only fitting to greet him in Russian. 'I've heard a great deal about you, *gospodin* Crimer,' she had said truthfully, for he had a brilliant professional reputation, 'and I look forward to working with you and learning from you.'

He had looked down at her coldly, making her uncomfortably aware of how petite she was. On such occasions, she would have loved to have been at least six foot tall. 'Well, I can't really return the compliment, Miss Romanova,' he had rudely answered in English. 'You see, I had really asked Leo Anders for an experienced United Nations interpreter, and all I get is someone I've never heard of. Well, I suppose you'll have to do.'

Galina bit her lip to refrain from bursting into tears of anger and frustration. There were a half dozen people or so in the room, and all eyes suddenly seemed riveted on her. 'Mr Crimer . . . ' she forced herself to say as evenly as she could.

'Ah, well, young lady, I'm glad to see you've decided to drop the *gospodin*. This is, after all, American territory and I understand you are American, despite your foreign-sounding name.'

Galina had to exercise utmost self-control not to slap him. 'Mr Crimer,' she continued as if nothing had happened, 'if you want me replaced, I suggest you contact Secretary General Anders. As far as I'm concerned, I'll be glad to go back to New York any time. But Mr Anders, whom I believe to be of sound judgement, sent me here to help you and I suggest before you contact him you find out if I can do the job. I have a feeling he might not appreciate being ordered about.'

An angry flush swept over Crimer's face. Uneasily, he turned to the rest of the group. 'Shall we go in to the briefing now?' he suggested hastily. 'We've got a lot of ground to cover before tomorrow. Ladies and gentlemen, this way to the auditorium, please.'

'Good for you,' whispered Tony Biddle, the Protocol man, to Galina as they filed down the corridor, 'he's one of the biggest bastards who's ever walked this earth. But watch it. You've made old creep Crimer mad, and he doesn't turn the other cheek.'

'Thanks for the warning, Tony. I'll be careful.' She could actually have thrown her arms around him out of sheer gratitude for his friendliness. She had met him just a couple of hours before, when he had picked her up at her hotel to bring her over to the briefing, but she already felt as if they had known each other for ages.

★   ★   ★

'Ladies and gentlemen,' began Basil Crimer from the lectern which stood on the dais facing the small semicircular auditorium, 'I think I need not emphasize the crucial historical importance of this first summit meeting between President Reagan and General Secretary Gorbachev. I think we are all aware that, in our own small way, we are helping to make history.'

'Pompous ass,' whispered Tony Biddle to Galina, who giggled like a schoolgirl. Crimer glowered at her and she could actually feel herself shrivelling up in her seat.

'As you know, the course of the meeting, the frequency and length of sessions are to be determined by the two leaders themselves and by no one else. Basically what I'm saying is that we, the interpreters servicing this summit, are going to be on call twenty-four hours out of twenty-four. It's rough, but it's part of the deal and a small price to pay for the privilege of being here.'

Does he drone on, thought Galina. Worse than a UN delegate. And I always believed they had mastered the art of talking without saying anything. But this man gets the prize for meaningless drivel. She looked around the auditorium, virtually empty except for herself, Tony Biddle, Crimer, a tall lady who Galina guessed must be Crimer's colleague from the State Department, and two Secret Service men.

'Our assignments will be as follows,' continued Crimer, at long last getting to the point. 'I will be doing all the meetings between the two leaders, assisted by my colleague Sandra Roth,' he indicated the tall handsome woman seated in the first row, 'with Sukhodrev, who is Gorbachev's personal interpreter, and Nikolai Golovin for the Soviet side. As is the custom in these bilateral talks, the Soviets will be working into English and we, the Americans, into Russian to ensure perfect comprehension of the source language.'

So where does that leave me, wondered Galina. He hasn't mentioned my name.

'As for you, Miss Romanova, you'll be doing some of the second-string meetings between Reagan's and Gorbachev's advisors, with Sandra and Mr Golovin helping you out as required.'

So there it is, thought Galina bitterly, he considers me strictly second-rate.

'I hope you can work into Russian, Miss Romanova,' continued Crimer implacably as all eyes in the room turned to stare at her as if she were a freak.

'As you know, Mr Crimer, at the UN we work into our mother tongue and mine happens to be English.'

'Well you'd better start practising your Russian hard and fast. I don't want any complaints about you from the delegation.'

Galina flushed a deep scarlet. Her impulse was to get up, run out of the auditorium, pack her bags and catch the first flight out to New York. But that would be giving in to Crimer, handing him his victory on a silver platter. And that would be the last thing she would do. 'There will be no complaints, Mr Crimer,' she forced herself to say loud and clear.

'Good. Now for the substance. You know that the core of the discussions will be taken up by the question of strategic arms reduction. Now the whole issue of intermediate and shorter-range missiles poses some formidable Russian-English terminology problems . . . '

* * *

The bar at the hotel Beau Rivage was just beginning to fill with early-evening customers when Galina walked in, with the firm intention of getting utterly drunk. The day's unpleasant events — that is, Basil Crimer's high-handed, arbitrary treatment of her — had depressed her more than she cared to admit.

Now that the meeting was over she felt tired, frustrated and lonely. She missed Bill's comforting presence, and she bitterly began to regret having accepted this assignment which so far seemed to have brought nothing but trouble. She also resented Basil Crimer's rather broad hint that she was incompetent to do a job the United Nations Secretary General had specifically selected her for.

She chose a corner table, as far as possible from a group of Arabs who seemed to be doing noisy and vehement business over endless glasses of Scotch. Briefly, she examined the drinks list and when the waiter came, ordered a double Stolichnaya on the rocks, aware it was going to be a killer and not caring. The first few sips had a more devastating effect than she would have imagined. Maybe it was the jet-lag. Filmy-eyed, she stared into her glass, brooding over her Russian roots and vaguely aware that she was becoming sentimental and maudlin. If only she knew someone in Geneva, someone to talk to, someone with whom she could share her untold sorrows.

She wondered where Nikolai was. At the Soviet Mission, probably, or out on the town with his compatriots. Why, she almost envied him, protected as he was by his position, by his society, by the Party. No doubt, despite all its restrictions, it was like an extended family, guaranteeing lifelong security in exchange for absolute loyalty to the system. One day maybe she would have the chance to ask him whether he ever felt as adrift as she did, tossed hither and thither like flotsam. I am a creature of accident, she had once said to her mother, things just happen to me. That had been after a brief and disastrous marriage she did her best to forget. It was even more true now that her parents were dead and she had absolutely no family left in the world. That was, she realized, the basic reason why she had drifted into her relationship with Bill, because she was no longer able to distinguish love from need. Bill had come to play an essential role, protecting her from all those predators who somehow sensed her desperate loneliness and vulnerability and preyed on it. Basil Crimer was one of those predators, but there had been others, men who had found it easy to humiliate her profession-ally and personally. At that moment,

Galina felt one of the world's victims.

'You seem awfully serious.' His voice so startled her that she nearly jumped out of her seat.

She looked at him blankly, as if he were an apparition. 'You do have a way of popping out of the blue, Nikolai Sergeevich.'

Nikolai smiled guilelessly. 'I know. Like a genie. *Mozhno?*' he asked, indicating the chair next to hers.

'Please do.' Despite herself, she was actually glad to see him. As soon as Nikolai sat down, the waiter rushed over. '*Un verre de Veuve Clicquot, s'il vous plaît,*' he ordered.

Galina's eyebrows went up. 'You certainly have expensive tastes.'

'So do you. That's Stolichnaya, isn't it?'

'Right. How do you know?'

'Because I've ordered it here several times. Pity they don't have good caviar to go with it, though.' Reaching into his pocket, he produced a pack of Dunhills and offered her one which he lit, she noticed, with a gold Cartier lighter. 'Cheers,' he said, raising his glass to her.

'*Za vashe zdorovye,*' she responded without enthusiasm, 'good health.'

'What a day,' he sighed, 'that briefing at our Mission just seemed to go on and on. *Kakaya skuka*. Such a drag. I suppose you had your own happening at the United States Mission.'

Galina nodded. 'Yes we did,' she answered irritably. She would just as soon have forgotten all about it.

'And tomorrow afternoon I've got to be at the airport to welcome our leader. I understand Reagan is arriving some time in the evening.'

'I don't know.' It was none of her business anyway. She was not going to be at the centre of things, like Nikolai. Thanks to Crimer, she would stay on the fringes of the summit. What the hell.

'Is something wrong?' he asked, watching her closely.

'Winter's getting me down,' she lied stupidly.

'Are you sure it's just winter,' he persisted, 'or is it something else?'

She smiled weakly. 'I'm going through a bad patch, that's all.'

'Isn't it interesting? So am I. Would you care to tell me about it?'

'Perhaps some other time. I'm exhausted and I've got to get a good night's sleep. So if you'll excuse me . . . '
She stood up, and he rose, which pleased her. She was not accustomed to such exquisite old-fashioned courtesy from American men.

'*Spokoynoy nochy*.' He shook her hand formally.

'Good night.'

'Will you have dinner with me some time?' he asked as Galina turned to go.

She looked at him more warmly than she meant to. 'I don't know,' she said very quietly. 'Call me and we'll see.'

5

Geneva, November 1985

Kurt von Steuben examined his mono-
grammed gold cufflinks carefully. They
had been a gift from his wife Anneliese
for their twentieth wedding anniversary,
and like everything else about his person,
they were conservative and slightly flashy
at the same time. He wiped an imaginary
speck of dust off his dark blue pin-striped
suit and contemplated his image in the
mirror. The suit went well with the silk
burgundy Dior tie and with his thick, neat
mane of silvery hair. He was, in one word,
distinguished, as befitted a man who held
the post of Director General of the
United Nations Office at Geneva.

Apparently satisfied with his image, he
turned away from the mirror and looked
at his wife, still fast asleep. She was lying
face down, her long blonde hair her sole
covering, for the sheet had slipped off her

60

lush naked body. Looking at her, he felt a sudden surge of warmth. Whether it was desire or sheer pride of ownership, he could not tell, for she was both a splendid mistress and an indisputable asset to him. At forty-two, she was still very attractive, with her full pouting lips and her firm, girlish figure. Granted, with her two sons grown and gone, she had plenty of time for swimming and tennis and dance-classes. His position called for a good deal of entertaining, and she did that well, so that he was grateful to her. Oh, he knew that a lot of men and the occasional woman shared her bed while he was away at the office or on mission, but it was a small price to pay for keeping their good solid partnership the going concern that it was.

Careful not to wake her, he tiptoed out of the room, closed the door softly and made his way down the curving staircase to the kitchen. He was pleased to see that the maid had left a pot of coffee on the hotplate for him. He poured himself a cup — black, no sugar — for at fifty he had suddenly realized he had to watch his figure. As he drank it, he gazed out of the tall windows that overlooked the carefully landscaped gardens around the house, and a wave of deep satisfaction swept through him. Even though this property in Cologny, one of the most exclusive areas of Geneva, had been bought largely with Anneliese's money, it was a fitting reflection of his current status, a harbinger of great things to come. When he became Secretary General of the United Nations — very soon, he hoped — they would move to New York and live in the official residence on Sutton Place, but no doubt Anneliese would want to keep this *residence de maître* with its swimming-pool and private pier for summer use.

Not bad, reflected Kurt von Steuben as he climbed into his white Mercedes and drove out of the garage, not bad for a middle class youth who had joined the United Nations as a very junior lawyer in the Human Rights Division twenty-five years before. Going to work for the UN Secretariat had seemed a good way to cover up his tracks in an Organization where no one took an uncomfortably close look at his past as a young SS officer during the *Anschluss*. In the *curriculum vitae* he drew up when he applied to the UN he had listed himself as an anti-Nazi activist, and that is what his official biography said to this day. It had been a snap, with no one questioning Kurt von Steuben's utter, complete devotion to the human rights ideals the Organization was believed to propound. No one, that is, until that meddlesome character Leo Anders — who happened to be Secretary General of the United Nations. How old Anders had found out was anybody's guess. What was done was done. It was now his job to make sure that no more skeletons came tumbling out of the cupboard.

Traffic was slow and heavy across the Pont de Mont Blanc, with police deployed everywhere. Von Steuben did not mind the long delay. It was, after all, the first day of the summit, and it gave him a thrill to think of the leaders of the two most powerful nations in the world, right here in the city where he lived and worked. Their arrival the day before had been a highly publicized media event, with the public's attention focused on Reagan and Gorbachev as much as on their stylish wives who vied with each other in elegance and glamour. Glamour is the right word for all this, thought the Director General, remembering that at the end of the week, he would be hosting a reception for the two leaders at his mansion in Cologny, which would shortly be combed by vast arrays of American and Soviet Secret Service men. While this intrusion into their privacy somewhat disturbed Anneliese, it did not inconvenience him in the least. The thrill of being so close to the centre of power was more than enough compensation for all the upheaval.

Besides, he reflected, Anneliese had better get used to it. As the wife of the United Nations Secretary General, she would be called upon to entertain world leaders and famous personalities regularly.

Dwelling on his ambitions, he thought of Basil Crimer. It was absolutely essential to arrange a meeting with him as soon as possible. In fact, it was becoming downright urgent, and he would have to be ultra discreet about it. They had to put the final touches to their master-plan. After that, it would be a question of timing, of waiting for the right opportunity to present itself. And he, Kurt von Steuben, believed it would. After all, he had been lucky most of his life.

By the time he reached the entrance to the *Palais des Nations*, where a uniformed guard saluted him respectfully, the Director General was in a state of barely controlled euphoria.

★ ★ ★

Later that day, just a few blocks from the *Palais des Nations*, at the Intercontinental Hotel, a meeting was in progress. The session, which had opened earlier that afternoon, was running late into the evening. At the horseshoe table, Galina was seated next to Max Kampelman, the brilliant chief American arms reduction negotiator. Across from her was Yuri Vorontsov, Kampelman's

Soviet counterpart with Nikolai at his side. The rest of the table was occupied by a bevy of advisors and secretaries busily following the exchange under way between the two negotiators.

' . . . and, as you know, the Soviet leadership is firmly opposed to any review of the provisions in the Anti-Ballistic Missile Treaty of 1972. You have also gathered that we are just as opposed to deployment of weapons in outer space. This is why we insist on your scrapping your Strategic Defense Initiative. To Star Wars we offer the alternative of Star Peace,' concluded Vorontsov, with a brief nod in Nikolai's direction.

Nikolai interpreted the statement into flawless English, only occasionally glancing at his notes, noticed Galina. She wished she could do as much, but she had to acknowledge her memory was no match for his so that she was virtually forced to read from her pad. She was, moreover, nervous. This was the first day of the summit and when she had reported to Crimer for her assignment that morning, he had told her to be at the

Intercontinental at four o'clock that afternoon and added, unnecessarily, 'I hope you'll live up to this,' which she had not even bothered to answer.

'We have taken note of your position,' Kampelman was saying, 'and while we agree there are many difficult issues to be resolved, we trust that the new openness of your leadership will help us make progress.'

It was Galina's turn to interpret and when she finished, she saw that Vorontsov was smiling broadly, obviously pleased by the American's flattering reference to Gorbachev's political reforms.

The two negotiators rose and warmly shook hands. The meeting was over at long last. It had been a tough bargaining session, with reams of extremely technical strategic weapons terminology to contend with, and Galina felt totally wrung out. Wondering what Crimer had in store for her, she felt a mild sense of triumph over him. Despite his repeated snide remarks, despite her extreme nervousness in the face of her first ever high-level meeting, she was reasonably satisfied with her day's work. She had coped well with the intricacies of interpreting into Russian, which she was not used to, and had conveyed an impression of being competent and relaxed, clearly earning the confidence of her listeners. She quickly collected her notes, which were to be shredded by a State Department secretary to ensure leak-proof secrecy, and headed for the door. She intended to stop by the shredding room to hand in her notes, then get back to her hotel and, after a light meal, go to bed. Tomorrow promised to be another full working day.

Nikolai caught up with her. '*Podozhdite*. Please wait.'

She stopped, puzzled. '*Da?*'

'Look, it's already nine o'clock and if you have no other plans I would like to invite you to dinner.'

'I . . . I don't know . . . ,' she said lamely.

'Don't hedge. Yes or no?'

'You are perceptive, aren't you?'

'Not especially. It's just that you are transparent. *Nu?*'

'Maybe you are used to bullying

women into accepting your invitations, maybe that's how you do it in your country, but in the West we are not used to being dragged off to dinner by our hair, you know.'

'I appreciate the lesson in Western manners. It would be useful if I had not spent a quarter of my life in the West. But I do admire your spirit. Now can we stop quibbling like two schoolchildren and start behaving a bit more maturely?'

'What do you want from me?'

'I told you. To take you out to dinner, talk to you over a relaxed meal, get to know you a bit better, Galina . . . ' He stopped in mid-sentence.

'Is something the matter?'

'I just realized I don't even know your patronymic.'

'Alexandrovna. Galina Alexandrovna.'

'Very well, Galina Alexandrovna . . . '

'Yes, Nikolai Sergeevich?'

Suddenly they both burst out laughing. 'Who do we remind you of?' asked Galina faking a serious tone.

'Two characters in a nineteenth-century Russian novel.'

'Exactly.'

'Why don't we drop the patronymics?'

'I couldn't agree more. I have always thought them an old-fashioned affectation anyway.'

'Now that that's settled, I repeat my question. Will you have dinner with me?'

'I am not sure it's such a good idea.'

'If what bothers you is that we might be seen together, I happen to know of a very small country inn which is much too modest for any of the people involved in this summit. There is also a big reception laid on for this evening at the Soviet mission, so most of them will be there.'

'You do prepare your ground, don't you?'

'Please?'

She sighed. '*Ladno*, Nikolai. I'll meet you down at the entrance in ten minutes. No, make it twenty,' she corrected herself, suddenly remembering the notes to be shredded and earnestly hoping no one had taken much notice of her exchange with Nikolai. It was unlikely, with so many aides and journalists hovering

70

about hungry for the merest scrap of news. Still, she had the disquieting impression she was being discreetly watched, and she felt guilty, as if she were about to cross into forbidden territory.

6

Geneva, November 1985

Galina sat in Nikolai's room at the Beau Rivage, listening to a tape of Vladimir Vissotsky's bitter satirical ballads about Soviet life and wondering what the devil she was doing there.

She had washed her dinner down with rather a lot of excellent dry local wine, which had prompted Nikolai to comment that there were some good things about Switzerland after all. As a result, they had become involved in endless debate about the relationship of wine to national character, laughed at themselves for being so Russian, and given up talking to drink some more. Galina was stunned to realize how well she felt with him, how familiar his words and gestures were, until it finally dawned on her that his exquisite use of the language and his clear intelligence reminded her of her father's.

Was that why she had accepted the invitation to round the evening off with a nightcap in his room? Had she done it to quench her nostalgia for her family, or her growing desire for Nikolai Golovin? Suddenly she became aware of the silence around her. The tape had stopped and Nikolai was looking at her as if he expected her to say something. The air hung heavy in the room, charged with the unspoken tension between them, making it hard for her to move or act normally.

Nikolai spoke first and his voice sounded strange, husky. 'Did you like his singing?' he asked, as the tape-recorder switched itself off with a loud click that seemed to reverberate in the room.

'Oh yes, very much. Is life in your country as miserable as he makes it out to be?'

Nikolai laughed. 'Pretty miserable, except for the Nomenklatura, the privileged caste.'

'Which you belong to?' She knew she was being blunt, but he had given her an opening and she had the feeling he

73

thought diplomacy was a stupid, simplistic game.

'You could say that.' His eyes were laughing, as if he were hugely enjoying a private joke.

'Well, aren't you afraid you might soon be losing some of these perks? I heard Gorbachev wanted to strip the ruling class of some of their privileges.'

'You mean like government limousines and travel abroad? I think he's absolutely right.'

'You mean it won't affect you?'

'No, it won't.'

'You are so sure of yourself.'

'Only of my usefulness, my dear Galina Alexandrovna. Do you know what they call people like me in the Soviet Union? *Prispsoblenniki* — conformists. It may not be very noble, but that is what I am and that is the secret of my success. Actually, both my wife and I are conformists. We have grasped that times have changed and that we must change with them if we are to stay on top.' Even as he mentioned Natalia, he cursed himself for bringing up the subject. It was an eerie sensation, as if he were driven by some sort of obscure guilt towards her, as if she were present in the room, jealous and vindictive, ever ready to poison his pleasure. *Chert yeyo deri*. To hell with her.

Galina was watching him with cool amusement, which he imagined to be at his expense. Little did he know that it was herself she was laughing at, herself and the whole situation, as banal as a cheap backstreet melodrama. The eternal triangle of absentee wife, unfaithful husband and potential mistress was so trite, even if the protagonists were American and Soviet international officials on a glamorous mission.

'So now you've brought the subject of your wife up, tell me about her, as I suppose you are dying to. Otherwise you wouldn't have mentioned her. So come on, what's she like?'

'Galina . . . '

She held up her hand. 'Please, Nikolai, I've been in enough of these situations with enough men. My wife doesn't understand me and all that. You know, the old tedious refrain. I would have thought you a bit more original, but obviously you are not. So let's get it over and done with. Besides, I'm really curious. So come on, what's she like?'

Nikolai shrugged, resigned. 'Beautiful, ambitious. A bit of an implacably efficient over-achiever. I suppose you could say she's a middle-aged Soviet version of your New York Yuppies.'

Galina laughed. 'It's a graphic enough description. What does she do?'

'She's a former Bolshoi prima ballerina who now works to promote Soviet-American cultural exchange. Does that satisfy your curiosity?'

'Not quite. There's another question I've been burning to ask you.'

'*Da?*'

'Do you feel you have strong roots?'

'*Ne ponial*. Sorry, I didn't follow.'

'You give me the impression that you and your wife are a team, a good team involved in the changes that are taking place in Soviet society. You have the blessing of the Party, to which you no doubt both belong, and all the perks of power. You love your country and you admire your leader and, by and large, you seem happy with your lot. Does that constitute roots?'

He shrugged. 'I suppose so. Why do you ask?'

'Because I don't have any, Nikolai. I'm a drifter and I was wondering what it was like to belong.'

'What about your family.'

'Dead.'

His eyebrows went up. 'All of them?'

'There weren't that many to begin with. Just my parents.'

'It must feel very lonely sometimes.'

'Yes.' Except for Bill, she added mentally, who has done a good deal to relieve that loneliness. She opened her mouth to tell Nikolai she had this boy-friend back in New York, this man who was sweet and loving and considerate, but changed her mind. She somehow felt that Bill was irrelevant to this moment, and hated herself for being so disloyal to the only man who had ever really loved her. Nikolai's voice cut into her thoughts, and it was as if she were suddenly answering a summons. His presence shut out the rest of the world, while Bill and New York faded like a passing dream.

'There are times when I am very lonely too, Galina.'

'What could possibly be missing from your life?'

'Tenderness. Can you understand that?'

She nodded and he held his arms out to her.

★　★　★

Months later, Galina would recall the first of her five nights with Nikolai Golovin as a vivid succession of images and impressions, none of them quite real and yet somehow imprinted on her. Once, in her student days at Columbia, she had written a paper on a poem that had struck her by its poignant beauty, and now she remembered it because it seemed to fit her affair with Nikolai perfectly. The flesh and the skin remember — it went — and old desire runs through the blood. Her flesh and her skin remembered him all right, even as his features and the sound of his voice began to fade from her. Her body carried the memory of his burning touch on the silky fabric of her dress, until her skin, taut with arousal, felt it would stretch and split open like parched earth. It remembered his lips brushing her breasts and his clever fingers beginning to know her, until a strange muffled cry that was like a lament tore from her throat and she begged him to enter her.

'Galya,' he whispered into her hair, 'Galochka.' And she felt the sting of tears at the sound of the old familiar diminutive of her name. It was the sound of home, long lost to her, found now for a fleeting moment, only to be lost again.

She clung to him, seeking shelter from the pain of her memories, and he held her close and still for a long time, because he had understood her constant sorrowing. Their lovemaking seemed to go on forever, caught in a dreamlike slow motion, interrupted and renewed, until their bodies cried out for a respite. 'You were hungry,' she said very quietly, as they lay side by side on crumpled sheets.

Absently, he traced the outline of her body with his finger. 'Natalia has had no time for love these past few years.'

'Do you have affairs while you are away on mission?'

'Sure. But nothing, oh nothing like this.'

'You are having me on.'

'No, Galya. Time is too short and you're quite special. I haven't come across anyone with your passion, Western or Soviet.'

'Nikolai, what's going to happen?'

'*Ne ponimayu.*'

'Of course you understand.'

'*Ne znayu*, Galochka. Or rather I do know, only too well. At the end of the summit on Saturday, I shall go back to Moscow and you to New York or wherever they send you next. Maybe one day we'll meet in Vienna or Delhi or Buenos Aires, maybe not. And you know that as well as I do, so why ask? Let's not start by hurting each other. There will be plenty of time for that.'

'Nikolai?'

'*Da, milaya?*'

'I'm starving.'

'What a coincidence. So am I.' And he covered her body with his.

★ ★ ★

Gaston Thevet considered himself fortunate, for the munificent Lord had made him rich, Swiss and unscrupulous. In Geneva, he was known to be the best chocolatier money could buy, supplying the diplomatic community and the well-heeled Genevois with first-rate chocolates from his elegant shop on the Rue du Rhône. It was also common knowledge that he was a dutiful and practising Calvinist, as well as a doting husband and father. That was Gaston Thevet's public face. His private face, so private that it was as well hidden from all as the dark side of the moon, was that of a spy for the same diplomatic community that sampled his highly prized confectionery. His detractors preferred to call him a well-paid errand boy, but Gaston Thevet indignantly rejected any such description of his second job.

He knew he had many detractors and, in fact, quite a few enemies who would have dearly loved to wring his neck and toss his earthly remains into Lake Geneva, but he felt entirely safe from any such vicissitudes. For he also knew that, as a servant to many masters, no one was ever sure Gaston Thevet would not betray him to a higher bidder. Very cleverly, he had founded his one-man secret service on the premise that international diplomacy is a dirty game and that sooner or later everybody would be snooping on everybody else. This inescapable truth constituted his business investment and his life insurance and Gaston Thevet rightly considered himself an excellent manager of both.

One blustery November morning, during a brief respite, Gaston Thevet was standing behind the counter in his shop, poring over his accounts with ill-disguised glee. With the Soviet — American summit in full swing, business had soared and he figured he would be able to afford the Ferrari his car dealer had been trying to sell him for the past few months.

His shining dreams of speed were momentarily interrupted by the door chime, signalling the presence of a customer. He looked up, forcing himself to smile. Fond as he was of making money, he could have welcomed a little rest, especially as his two assistants were away sick and he was left alone to run the business during an unusually crowded week.

The newcomer was wearing a thick overcoat and a homburg which, to Gaston Thevet's sharp sartorial eye, typecast him as Eastern European. He was not mistaken.

'Monsieur Thevet,' he began with a heavy Russian accent.

'*Moi-même*,' said Gaston amiably, sniffing good business.

'I come on behalf of Orel. I believe you have worked for him before.'

'*Bien sûr.*' Indeed, he remembered many assignments for Rudenko, Deputy Chief of the KGB, code-named Orel, the Eagle.

'We want you to follow someone. You report to me. How much?'

'Depends on the quarry.'

'Nikolai Golovin, Soviet interpreter at this summit.'

Gaston Thevet was puzzled. 'Why don't you do it yourselves? *Vous avez les ressources*.'

'Too obvious. You would be, so to say, less conspicuous, yes?'

'True. But I must warn you my rates have gone up. Cost of living keeps rising, you know. Geneva is one of the most expensive cities in the world.'

'How much?'

'How long is the assignment?'

'Until the end of the week, when Golovin goes back to Moscow.'

'It will cost you fifty thousand francs, plus expenses.'

'*Très bien*.'

'Just one question. Why do you want him tracked?'

'He's seeing an American colleague, a woman named Galina Romanova.' The Russian's lip curled in pure disdain for Nikolai Golovin's poor taste.

Gaston Thevet's mouth began to water. This promised to be meaty. An American called Galina Romanova, eh? Probably of Russian emigré stock, having an affair with a Soviet. He knew someone at the United States mission who would find this sweet little love intrigue very, very interesting.

★   ★   ★

In the half-darkness, Galina whispered, 'Will I hear from you?'

Nikolai stroked her hair, which lay across the pillow like a silver stream. 'I doubt it.'

'I'll come and visit you in Moscow then. I'll sign up for one of those six-week courses at the Institute for Foreign Languages and meet you every day on a deserted street corner.'

'I can just see you, blending into the Soviet crowd. They would spot you as a foreigner a mile away.'

'Do I look so Western?'

'Not just Western, *dorogaya*. American.'

'And you look Georgian. I thought so the very first time I met you, in Anders' office. Was it really last week? It seems ages ago.'

'Doesn't it? And this is our second night together. It calls for a celebration.' And he reached for the Dom Perignon which stood in a silver bucket by the bed. He had had it delivered ice-cold just before she joined him in his room. Why was it in his room, not hers, that they kept their trysts, he wondered, but let the thought pass. It struck him that she was remarkably unconcerned about the problems their affair was bound to cause her. Strange girl, self-possessed and forlorn at the same time.

'You haven't answered my question.'

'Which question? I'm sorry, I forgot.' He poured her a glass of champagne. '*Za vashe zdorovye.*'

'Are you Georgian?'

'My mother was. That's why she was spared by Stalin.'

'And your father?'

'He was a Russian officer. He was sent to a concentration camp after he was returned by the Germans. He was a prisoner of war, and his crime had been to surrender instead of getting himself killed. Millions, including the writer Solzhenitzyn suffered in the *batyushka*'s iron grip. The little father did not forgive.' His voice was sharp, bitter.

'I feel grateful my family was spared that.'

'When did they leave Russia?'

'When the Revolution broke out. My grandparents did. My parents were small children then. They grew up in exile.'

'And you have a displaced person's soul, right?'

'Somewhat.'

'Is that why you are here, with me?'

She shrugged. 'Maybe. I don't really know.'

'You might lose your job if they find out.'

'I'll find another one, or maybe I'll write a book. Yes, why not? A novel about us. I'm sure it would make the top ten in the *New York Times Book Review*.'

'Sounds good. Will you send me a copy?'

'Several, if you want, for distribution among your colleagues at the Foreign

Ministry. And you can also give a copy to . . . '

His kiss stopped her in mid-sentence.

★   ★   ★

In his office at the American Mission, Basil Crimer was working late, writing up the verbatim record of that afternoon's meeting between the President and the General Secretary. The interpreters for the two leaders reconstructed the highly confidential record from their own notes on the talks in a room especially assigned for the purpose at the offices of the United States mission. It was the rule that two Marines stood guard while this work was in progress and the record would then go into a safe to which only top aides knew the combination.

Basil Crimer was tired and frustrated. He considered this to be menial secretarial work, and his only consolation was that he would soon stop doing it. When he and Kurt von Steuben carried out their big plan, his fate would turn. No more round-the-clock work. An interpreter, even a high-level one like himself, is no more than a glorified servant, at the beck and call of delegations, he reflected bitterly. Well, soon, very soon, he would show these State Department bastards a thing or two. When he took up his appointment at the UN under von Steuben, he would run the show.

The phone on his desk rang. He picked it up, annoyed at the interruption. All he wanted was to finish his work and go home.

'*Monsieur Crimer? Gaston Thevet à l'appareil.*'

'*Qui?*'

'Gaston Thevet. You don't know me, Monsieur, but I know you.'

Basil Crimer was torn between his curiosity and his desire to slam the phone down. In the end, his curiosity won out. 'How do you know me?'

'I make it my business to know everybody in this town.'

'What do you want?' Crimer asked irritably. The man must be some sort of charlatan. He felt vaguely uneasy.

'To give you some information.'

Crimer looked up at the two young Marines, who stood as still as a pair of dummies in a shop window. How much had they heard and remembered, he wondered. He could not possibly talk here without compromising himself.

'Monsieur Crimer?'

'Yes.'

'Are you interested?'

What if the man really did have something? He would not know for certain unless they met. 'All right, Mr Thevet,' he said, 'let's have lunch tomorrow. Café de la Paix, one o'clock.'

7

Geneva – Moscow, November 1985

For the tenth time that evening, Basil Crimer reread the gold-embossed invitation to the formal reception and dinner to be hosted that Wednesday evening, November 26th, by the UN Director General in honour of their Excellencies President Reagan of the United States and General Secretary Gorbachev of the Soviet Union. He fingered the card lovingly, then set it back on the desk as if it were a fragile piece of priceless crystal. There was no doubt about it, he was beginning to travel in fancy circles. He buttoned his silk shirt and glanced at his watch, the latest Patek Philippe model, just purchased at Baume et Mercier in Geneva. Life could be good, very good indeed, he thought, lighting a cigarette and inhaling deeply, contentedly. It seemed especially good when you had started life out as the son of poor Russian emigré intellectuals. His parents had, of course, given him a first rate education, but the rest he had done himself. Even marriage to La Donnia had been his own doing. The stupid old cow. She still had hot pants for him, after all these years, and once in a while he would oblige, keeping her interest in him alive. There was, after all, her money which came in regularly every month and enabled him to stay in the very choicest hotels, which he could never have afforded on his mere State Department allowance.

It was still early — six o'clock, and the reception was not until eight. He had time for a glass or two of the first-class champagne from the minibar in his suite. He opened the fridge and poured himself the contents of a small bottle of Kruger. You had to hand it to the management of the President Hotel — they kept you well supplied with the best champagne money could buy. Trouble was, he had to watch his drinking, because he would probably have to do some interpreting at von Steuben's reception — after-dinner toasts, improvised speeches, all that babble. Well, if all went according to plan, he would soon be invited to high-level parties without having to sing for his supper. He could not wait for that day to come.

That evening, he would no doubt be teamed up with that Soviet golden boy, Nikolai Golovin, who was rumoured to be Gorbachev's personal buddy. They were two of a kind, reflected Crimer with contempt, just a pair of Soviet wolves in Western clothing. He knew their type all right, the type that had ruthlessly robbed his grandparents of everything they possessed, sending them out of Russia into endless exile. What he could not understand was a bitch like that Galina Romanova, sleeping with Golovin. How could she do it with a Soviet? She was attractive all right, he would not have minded her himself, but she had to be a nymphomaniac to go for Golovin, or for any Soviet for that matter.

Crimer had it on good authority that Romanova and Golovin were sleeping together, if Gaston Thevet's evidence was anything to go by. The chocolatier had not been able to produce anything specifically incriminating about the couple, like pictures or tapes, but his men, disguised as waiters and busboys, had followed Romanova and Golovin closely enough to have seen Galina leaving his room at the Beau Rivage. For his skimpy evidence, Thevet asked for an advance, and promised more concrete proof the next time he met Crimer. There was something about the shop-keeper/spy that bothered Basil, something that kept tugging uncomfortably at the back of his mind. He rightly supposed Thevet's motives to be purely pecuniary, for he himself full well knew that money breeds the desire for more money. But it was the man's personality he could not fathom, and it left him feeling ill at ease. Thevet had shifty eyes that kept darting in all directions, as if he expected someone to come into the room any moment, and shifty, nervous fingers that offered a limp, moist handshake. He was, thought Crimer, altogether treacherous. A disturbing thought crossed his mind. If Thevet did indeed know absolutely everything about absolutely everybody in Geneva, then he was probably aware of Crimer's relationship with von Steuben. And that was something neither of them could well afford. Crimer sighed heavily. How to dispose of Thevet was something he would have to discuss with his friend Kurt at the party, one more item on an agenda which promised to be filled to the brim.

He braced himself for what he knew would be a very full evening.

* * *

Even by her own exacting standards, Anneliese von Steuben looked stunning. In her low-cut black velvet sheath set off by a belt of blue and white rhinestones, her thick long mane of ash-blond hair falling in gentle waves down to her shoulders, she had undeniable star quality. Trouble was, she reasoned, she could not afford to be a star that evening without outshining the two First Ladies, Mrs Reagan and Mrs Gorbachev, both known to be superbly elegant women who did not take kindly to female competition. The last thing Anneliese wanted to do was to hinder her husband's career at the very reception which was supposed to advance it.

She turned away from the swivel mirror where, for the past five minutes, she had been studying herself in the most painstaking detail, and went to her dresser. Carefully, she opened the heavy pearl-encrusted jewellery box that had been brought by special courier that afternoon from the bank vault where it spent most of the year, to be retrieved only on very, very special occasions.

Anneliese loved that box, which had been a wedding gift from her mother, herself a great beauty and prominent socialite in the glitter of pre-war Vienna and, some said, even after the *Anschluss*, when her home, Schloss Grunwald, was reputedly open to high-level German officers. Whenever any hint of her family's pro-Nazi sympathies cropped up, Anneliese wrote extensive disclaimers in newspapers, for she would not accept any maligning of her late parents' reputation. Lately, though, the press had left her people alone, choosing her husband as a target instead. Anneliese had indulged in bouts of self-righteous indignation, but Kurt had prevailed on her to lie low and quiet. Ignore these allegations, he had argued, and they will go away. She herself doubted it, because she knew that when the press latched on to a public figure's undisclosed past, it was like a dog with a tired old bone. It just would not let go. Well, she would not upset herself over these little things now, for she had to make sure she looked her best and tension was the natural enemy of beauty. She opened the box and selected a pair of chunky sapphire and diamond pendants which she clipped on. She was about to pick up the matching necklace, when she changed her mind. Too much jewellery would make her look like a Christmas tree, and she knew vulgarity was unforgivable in the future UN Secretary General's wife.

There was a light knock on the door. '*Entrez*,' snapped Anneliese irritably. It was probably Mitzi, her maid, who had crowned the whole difficult day by upsetting a priceless vase over her mistress's equally priceless Chinese carpet. Without a moment's hesitation, Anneliese had given the wretched creature notice, disregarding the girl's record of eight years' impeccable service. Not nearly impeccable enough, though, for Anneliese expected nothing less than perfection from her terrified staff.

The door opened and, instead of the unhappy Mitzi, it was a self-confident, radiant Kurt von Steuben who walked in. He went up to his wife and stood behind her, placing his hands on her shoulders. 'You look exquisite, *liebling*,' he said appreciatively. Even after nearly twenty-five years of marriage, the sight of Anneliese's beauty cut his breath short. 'I am proud of you.'

She whirled around to face him, an anxious expression on her face. 'Oh Kurt, I do hope it's going to go all right. You've no idea. These past hours have been a nightmare. The kitchen staff was in an uproar because Fauchon was late delivering the truffles, I thought I would have to go out there and face the President and the General Secretary in curlers because the man Carita sent from Paris to do my hair missed his plane. Mitzi has been making a mess of things and . . . What's so funny?'

'You, my darling, you. Everybody knows you are the perfect hostess, so nothing can go wrong when you throw a party, even a reception of these proportions.'

'Have you any idea, Mr Director General, what it takes to plan an evening for two hundred choice guests?'

'A lot. But you can do it. I have full confidence in you, Mrs von Steuben. Besides, you'd better get used to it. As the Secretary General's wife, you will have even bigger receptions in store for you.'

She rewarded him with a radiant smile. 'Well, I'm glad to tell you everything's finally under control. And now, we'd better go. I want to give the dining-room a quick once-over before the Secret Service arrive.'

★ ★ ★

Anneliese barely had time to run her expert eye over the twenty circular tables set with her best Limoges china and Baccarat crystal. With the practised efficiency of a hostess used to diplomatic receptions, she inspected the place settings, the tablecloths, serviettes and fresh tea roses, her favourite flowers, especially grown for her in a greenhouse near by. It was Anneliese's habit to fill her house with masses of tea roses even in the dead of winter, regardless of cost, and she used them lavishly at her receptions, for they were elegant enough to be ornamental and neutral enough not to offend anyone's taste. The choice of flowers had been easier than the selection of a menu for tonight. For months, her staff had been boning up on every scrap of information concerning the Reagans' and the Gorbachevs' taste in food and drink and Anneliese had carefully pored over their findings. The result had been a simple but classy menu: black Sevruga caviar washed down with Stolichnaya vodka, salmon mousse and the white wine she favoured for its lightness — Gewurtztraminer — veal with truffles in a delicate cream sauce accompanied by California Cabernet Sauvignon red, crepe suzette with a variety of sweet fillings, less fattening than the usual run of desserts — Mrs Reagan and Mrs Gorbachev were rumoured to be keen figure-watchers, much like herself, so she sympathized.

Anneliese was closely scrutinizing the head table which was supposed to accommodate herself, her husband, the two guests of honour and their wives, when the Secret Service made their entrance, immediately followed by Gorbachev's bodyguards. For what seemed like an eternity, Soviets and Americans danced a clever choreography around each other, combing the dining room as if it were a piece of mined enemy territory. They all but ignored Anneliese, who was getting used to their presence — they had been in and out of her house for weeks now, inspecting its every nook and cranny.

Far from objecting, she was, in fact, rather pleased the agents were still there when her first guests arrived — it was an indication of the high-level character of the evening. Basil Crimer walked in and formally kissed Anneliese's hand. Although they knew each other well, he carefully wanted to avoid any impression of familiarity in public.

'And where is our Director General?' he asked jovially.

'My husband will be here any minute.'

'It's quite a gathering you've got here tonight, *gnädige Frau*.'

She smiled modestly. 'We do what we can. Ah, here's Kurt. Will you excuse me while I attend to my other guests?'

'But of course, Madame.' He bowed courteously, took a glass of champagne from a tray proffered by a passing waiter, and acknowledged Kurt von Steuben, who had just joined them. 'Good evening, it's an honour to be here tonight.'

'Mr Crimer, I am so glad you could come. I do hope you enjoy the party. I am afraid it's going to be a bit of a busman's holiday for you.'

'You know, Mr von Steuben, I've always been an admirer of your excellent English. You can't even leave it to us linguists to do that well. You outstrip all of us.'

Smarmy bastard, thought von Steuben, who did not trust Crimer as far as he could throw him, probably with good reason. He knew his sentiments were fully reciprocated by Basil, also with sound reason. They needed each other, that was all. They were welded together by the most intoxicating of drives — power — and they well knew they would soon be too far gone to dispense with each other.

Since their meeting years before at an international conference where von Steuben headed the Austrian delegation and Crimer was a member of the interpretation team, their need and their contempt for each other had grown and ripened on fertile soil.

'I have to talk to you,' said Crimer under his breath, though he was sure their conversation would be drowned out by the hubbub of conversation. The room had filled up with guests.

'I told you, not now,' answered von Steuben, ignoring the urgency in the other man's voice.

'Aside from our project, there is another matter that . . . '

Von Steuben cut him off short. 'I told you, not now. When the summit is over.'

'But Kurt . . . '

'Basil, don't be dumb. Come and have dinner with us two weeks from today. Ah, Mr Ambassador, how are you? So pleased to have you . . . '

And von Steuben turned away to greet an immensely tall African, majestic in his bright flowing robes, who added yet another picturesque touch to a reception featuring guests in a myriad variety of national costumes.

Crimer felt frustrated and angry. Though he sympathized with von Steuben's caution, he had not expected an abrupt brush-off. Maybe all this notoriety, and the promise of more, was going to the Director General's head. Well, he, Basil Crimer, would soon remind Mr Kurt von bloody Steuben where his true allegiances lay. For openers, he would get rid of Thevet on his own. He had planned to discuss the whole matter with von Steuben, but the man obviously had no time for him tonight. That was just too bad, but there were certain matters that could not wait. Across the room, he spotted Nikolai Golovin, chatting to a group of Soviet diplomats. That reminded him. Before Thevet disappeared for good, he would have to extract some evidence concerning Galina Romanova and Nikolai Golovin, specific evidence that would go into Romanova's file at the United Nations, to be used in due course.

★　★　★

Suddenly, as if on cue, a hush fell over the two hundred people assembled in the von Steubens' drawing room. A detachment of Secret Service men entered and fanned out in all directions, followed by their faithful Russian colleagues. Kurt and Anneliese von Steuben made their way to the entrance, just as two black limousines, bearing the American and Soviet flags respectively and flanked by motor-cycle outriders, drew up outside the door. President Reagan emerged from the first car, followed by his wife Nancy, resplendent in an emerald-green gown and a ranch-mink coat, both, Anneliese guessed, by Galanos, Mrs Reagan's favourite designer. Secretary General Gorbachev and his wife, Raisa, stepped out of the second limousine, and Anneliese thought how well-deserved Mrs Gorbachev's reputation for elegance was. The Soviet First Lady, dressed by the master couturier Vyacheslav Zaitsev, looked far younger than her years in an off-white evening dress and dark brown sable cape. The two star couples greeted each other, to the applause of the other guests, and made their way towards the von Steubens. Innumerable flash bulbs popped, cameras rolled, and everybody had the distinct and thrilling impression of being on a movie set. This was the only part of the evening on which Anneliese authorized news coverage, thinking in no small measure of the publicity she and her husband would be deriving from the event.

★   ★   ★

In her room at the Beau Rivage, Galina was watching an evening news flash on the reception given by the von Steubens for the visiting leaders of the two world superpowers. She had not been invited, nor had she expected to be. Nikolai, of course, had been asked and so had Crimer. Despite a twinge of regret at being left out, like a child excluded from a play group, she did not really mind. She was exhausted from work-related pressures, from her unfortunate relationship with Crimer and from her affair with Nikolai, which she found emotionally and physically draining.

★   ★   ★

There was another woman watching the same report, a woman who was neither exhausted nor indifferent. She was, in fact, downright livid at the thought of missing the party, in fact the whole summit week in Geneva. When the commentator on *Vremya*, the main Moscow evening news programme, began to describe the glittering occasion in minute detail, giving a great deal of play to Mikhail and Raisa Gorbachev, it was all Natalia Golovin could do to prevent herself from smashing the damn television set to smithereens.

8

Moscow – Geneva, November 1985

Arkady Rudenko was caught in the eye of the storm. He knew, moreover, that the going could get rough, especially when the storm happened to be called Natalia Golovin.

'*Svoloch!*' she yelled. 'You first-class lazy bastard! What do you think you are doing? Just how dare you insult my intelligence by bringing me these? *Kak ty smeesh*, eh?'

'*Natasha, yspokoisia pozhalusta . . .* '

'Don't you go and tell me to calm down, *durak*, when you've gone and botched everything once more!' She picked up a heavy Murano vase and hurled it on the floor, where it promptly and predictably smashed to bits.

The Deputy Chief of the KGB made himself even smaller on the sofa where he was sitting, well out of the line of fire.

Impervious, Natalia continued her tirade, liberally interspersed with volleys of insults. 'You pea-brain, I ask you to bring me concrete evidence of Nikolai Golovin's infidelity, and these amateur pictures are the best you can do. Is this what the State pays you for, Arkady? Is this what we, decent Soviet citizens, spend our money on, to feed you and your bunch of imbecile pigs who cannot even take a picture properly, as any five-year-old could do?'

Arkady Rudenko opened his hands in a gesture of desperate resignation. There was absolutely nothing he could say because he knew she had touched on a sore spot. Unfortunately, he had to agree with her. The job was amateurish. Whoever had taken the photographs of Galina Romanova going into Golovin's room at the Beau Rivage either did not know the first thing about photography or needed his telephoto lens changed. The result had been a blurred, faint picture of a figure, barely recognizable as a woman standing in front of a door with supposedly a number on it, which had come out as a grey spot. It proved exactly nothing.

As for the tapes of Romanova's and Golovin's meetings, Rudenko had not even dared bring them, for they were worse than useless. All they produced was the most deafening silence — Golovin, concluded Rudenko, must have very cleverly scrambled them, which in turn meant Thevet's boys had planted the bugs in places which were all too visible. He was furious with himself for using that bastard Thevet, who owed him some explaining. The chocolatier had probably tried to save money by using cheap local talent, pocketing the difference.

All in all, he reflected wearily, things had gone badly for him that evening. He had tried to placate Natalia by bringing her a bottle of Chivas Regal that he had bought on his recent trip to Western Europe and now he fervently wished he had kept it, for it might well have been his last opportunity to buy Scotch or anything else abroad, if Natalia had her way with the higher-ups. As soon as she had opened the door to him, he knew he was in dire danger. In her long Moroccan caftan, she looked like some kind of wild, untamable Circassian of the Steppes. He recognized the signs of imminent explosion from the way her long fingers twisted the heavy gold chain that hung down to her slender waist and, with a pang of nostalgia, he remembered those long nights of lovemaking with her long ago, when she used to claw the skin of his naked back until she drew blood. He wholeheartedly wished he could have her right there and then but, if there was the slightest doubt left as to her disposition, she proceeded to dispel it immediately. 'Get out of here, you useless bum! *Negodnik!*' she spewed. 'I swear to you by everything I hold dear that as soon as Mikhail Sergeevich and Raisa Maximovna return from Geneva, I'll have you hauled before the authorities on charges of utter incompetence, corruption, and embezzlement of State funds. Comes at the right time too, with Gorbachev's anti-corruption drive, you'll be made an example of. I'll have you strung up, Arkady Rudenko, I promise you that, so help me God! And now, out of here, *von!*'

He hoped she did not notice his violent tremor as he stood up and scrambled out of her apartment as fast as his tired old legs could carry him. If she could prove her charges, he would have had it. He should have gone to Geneva himself, instead of leaving the whole thing to that fool Oleg Glupoff of the Soviet mission to the United Nations. In turn, Glupoff had contacted Thevet, who had made a mess of things. Yes, he thought as he ran down the stairs, a little vacation in Switzerland would have been nice. In fact, he wished he were there right now.

Behind him, he heard the sound of an object violently smashing on Natalia's door. Pity about that bottle of Chivas Regal. What a waste.

★   ★   ★

It seemed to Galina that her affair with Nikolai was over almost before it began, and, ironically, that the end was far better than the beginning. Their last lovemaking was sublime, maybe because it was the

113

last, with their bodies blending together in such perfect rhythm, that they truly seemed to have been made for each other and for each other alone. They drove each other wild with their caresses, as if performing a crazy dance choreographed by an inspired artist. Nikolai possessed her repeatedly, and with such force and intensity as if he were really seeking to imprint himself on her very soul, to make sure she would never forget him as long as she lived.

Outside, the rain had been falling steadily all night. Presently, the air had begun to fill with the street noises of dawn, with the honking of early trucks and cars, with the busy and purposeful steps of all those good Swiss citizens hurrying to work at daybreak.

The end had come.

Nikolai got up, poured himself a brandy and, not trusting himself to look at her, said very quietly, 'It's time, Galya. Get dressed and go, please.'

Why is it that all backstreet affairs seem to end on a cold winter dawn, she thought grimly. With her back to him, almost as if embarrassed, she began to pick up her clothes, which in his impatience he had torn off her the night before.

Dressed, she stood before him and, to no avail, struggled to check the tears that were spilling down her cheeks. She felt a sense of deep loss, one more in the wave of relentless losses that marked her life.

'I suppose it's pointless to hope for another . . . '

He shook his head sadly. 'Totally. There's absolutely no place for this in our lives, and you know that.'

She nodded. 'This morning, we'll be working together.'

'Yes, as if nothing had ever happened between us.'

'I really wish we didn't have to face each other in a conference room.'

'Believe me, so do I, but it seems unavoidable. And now, Galya, go, please . . . '

Helplessly, she fell into his arms. Tenderly, he kissed her hair, her neck, her open, eager mouth and, shocked, he felt an overwhelming desire for her welling up in him. He tightened his grip on her, but she fought him, and he let her go.

'It's not fair, Nikolai.'

'*Prosti menia*. Please forgive me, for a moment I lost control.'

'*Do svidanya, Nikolai.*'

'*Do svidanya, Galya.*'

Without looking back, she ran out of the room and out of his life.

★ ★ ★

A security guard checked Galina's pass and waved her through, into the lobby of the Intercontinental which, on that last day of the historic summit, was about as restful as Grand Central Station during the rush-hour. As far as the eye could see, harried officials seemed engaged in transporting masses of documents, while chain-smoking reporters, their eyes red from lack of sleep, occupied every available phone.

A quick glance in the mirror told Galina that she looked good, despite a sleepless night and emotional strain. She was freshly made up, her long hair was brushed back in an attractive layered style, and her light grey suit and cream silk blouse were sober yet feminine. Just as well. She would have to withstand the merciless eye of television cameras and the hot glare of spotlights for as long as the press conference lasted. It was to be the last joint public appearance of US Secretary of State George Schultz and Soviet Foreign Minister Eduard Shevardnadze, an occasion second only to the press conference to be given later that Friday by President Reagan and General Secretary Gorbachev.

As she walked into the room, Galina wondered why Crimer had assigned her to a meeting of that importance. Was it because he was confident he would trip her up if she misinterpreted out of sheer nervousness? Or did he suspect something about her relationship with Nikolai Golovin, and would he gloat over her uneasiness at having to work with him that morning? Whatever the man's reasons were, she would always doubt his intentions. For some mysterious motive, Basil Crimer was gunning for her and she

117

had the uncanny feeling his hostility would not end with the Geneva meeting.

She took her seat at the back of the podium and eyed the empty chair next to her as if it were on fire. In a few minutes, Nikolai would be sitting there, and she prayed for self-control with all her might. It was such a relief to realize that, in two days, she would be back in New York, back in her comfortable routine of UN meetings and dates with Bill. Almost as if Geneva had never happened.

A very blond, very shy young man walked up to the chair next to hers and sat down. She stared at him, trying to hide her amazement and obviously not succeeding because he said, almost apologetically, 'I am Alexei Filatov. I have been sent to replace Nikolai Golovin, who has another meeting this morning.'

Another meeting? But, she wanted to answer, there are no other meetings scheduled this morning. You mean, he has got himself replaced or else your authorities decided for him. Whatever it is, wherever he is, I shall never know, she thought helplessly. Nikolai had disappeared with the same suddenness as he had appeared in Leo Anders' office exactly one week before.

In the room, the crowd of reporters fell silent. Gradually, the buzz of voices died down as if the lights had suddenly dimmed and the show were about to begin.

Preceded by a flurry of aides, Secretary of State Schultz and Foreign Minister Shevardnadze walked in, clearly in an excellent mood. The two men were obviously satisfied with the results of the summit for which they had largely laid the groundwork, thought Galina. They seemed jovial and friendly and brimming with the self-confidence stemming from a job well done.

As soon as they were seated, with Galina and Alexei behind them, an aide handed the Secretary of State a prepared statement. 'Ladies and gentlemen, Foreign Minister Shevardnadze and I are pleased to report that the first summit meeting between our two leaders has been an unqualified success. Of course, areas of difference remain, particularly as regards the strategic arsenals of our two countries, but our negotiators here in Geneva will press on to reach an early agreement on these and other issues, particularly the prospects for the signature of the Intermediate Nuclear Forces Treaty during the visit by General Secretary Gorbachev to Washington next year.'

He paused and signalled for the interpretation. '*Dami i gospoda . . .* ,' began Galina.

* * *

The press conference was mercifully over and so, for all intents and purposes, was her assignment in Geneva. As she threaded her way through the corridors packed with journalists and officials, she pondered the past week, a whole eternity packed into seven days. On balance, she did not regret having accepted Leo Anders' assignment, which any of her New York colleagues would have gladly pounced upon. She smiled at the thought of the envious glances she would draw when she walked into the office on Monday morning, and they would never know the half of it, that half which had been her secret garden shared with Nikolai Golovin. Most women, she realized, would have been happy to sleep with Nikolai, and most men, to talk to him, and she had done both and was all the richer for it. Even now, her body still wanted him and rebelled against the idea that it was all over for good, though her mind commanded her to put the affair behind her, turning it into a memory from now on. It would be her own very private memory, never to be discussed with anyone, and its very secrecy would be a way of preserving Nikolai and what they had had together in her heart untouched by the passage of time.

She had been so absorbed in her thoughts, so totally oblivious to the outside world, that she violently collided with Basil Crimer. The impact nearly toppled them both off their feet. Galina mumbled an apology which he ignored. 'Can't you even look where you are going?' he yelled, making a few heads turn.

She flushed crimson. 'Mr Crimer, I said I was sorry. I'm very tired and . . . '

It was as if the encounter had lanced a boil that had been festering inside him all week, so that all his venom came pouring out. 'Tired,' he spewed, 'you have the nerve to tell me you are tired. Well, it can't be from work, can it? More like it, you've been partying like crazy here, so that next morning you were too damn exhausted to produce a decent piece of work.'

'What do you mean?' He could not possibly have have known about her and Nikolai. But then again, why not? After all, they had been constantly seen together around the Intercontinental and the Beau Rivage, and Crimer was far from stupid. He could have easily put two and two together, adding up to a case of clear double bluff.

'Come on, my dear Miss Romanova, don't you play the little girl lost with me. I suggest you save your act for fascinating and mysterious Soviets like Nikolai

Golovin,' he answered nastily.

'Gospodin Crimer,' she said quietly, switching to Russian, which he clearly did not deign use with her. 'I forbid you to insinuate . . . '

'You forbid me,' he cut her off rudely, 'and who are you to forbid me, you mediocrity? I don't know what Leo Anders was thinking of, sending you here. From the start, I knew he had made a big mistake, and I'll make sure he knows it. Not only are your morals dubious . . . '

'Prove it, Mr Crimer, prove it.'

'Oh I will, believe you me.'

'You mean you would dearly love to but you can't.' With relish, she saw that she had the upper hand now.

'What I can prove, though, is your incompetence as an interpreter. I've been told that this morning you translated Intermediate Nuclear Forces as *Promezhutochnye* whereas you ought to have known that the official Soviet terminology is not a literal translation of the American. If you had boned up on your documents you would have known that in Soviet parlance the Intermediate Nuclear forces are called Medium and Shorter-Range Missiles . . . '

To his utter amazement, she just turned and walked away from him, leaving him standing in the middle of the lobby, his mouth open in mid-sentence. A few people who had witnessed the end of the scene snickered and Basil Crimer went scarlet with rage. No one had ever done this to him. No one had ever dared ridicule him in public. The bitch, he mumbled, the goddamn Soviet-lovin' bitch, she'll pay me for this, and how.

* * *

Back in her hotel, Galina felt as if a storm had washed over her, leaving her totally drained, beached like a hollow shell. Wearily, she made her way to the elevator. All she needed now was some sleep, after which she would start packing and get out of here and back to New York. She had to see Leo Anders before the Secretary General heard second-hand distorted reports on her work in Geneva, and she had overheard Crimer saying that

124

he was leaving for Washington on Saturday night. Her own flight to New York was on Sunday morning, so if she made it to the office early on Monday . . .

'Mademoiselle Romanova, Mademoiselle Romanova.'

She turned and saw a bell-hop rushing towards her.

'*Oui?*'

'*Télégramme pour vous.*'

Who on earth could be sending her a cable? She honestly hoped it was not Bill, announcing his arrival in Geneva to spend the week-end with her. She badly needed to be alone, to collect her thoughts, so that she could pull herself together and face the world once again. With trembling fingers, she opened the telegram, and her eyes widened as she ran through its contents. 'Your assignment in Geneva is extended indefinitely,' it read. 'Please report to the Chief Interpreter at the Palais des Nations on Monday, December 2nd.'

9

Geneva – Moscow, November 1985

The night air was cool and crisp with the promise of imminent snow as Basil Crimer crossed the bridge over the river Arve — noting the spot carefully for later reference — into the old neighbourhood of Carouge. He glanced at the luminous dial of his watch and stepped up his pace. It was a quarter to eight and he was meeting his date, who was Swiss and therefore punctual, at eight o'clock sharp, and he simply could not afford to be late.

Sometimes, like tonight, he was reluctantly forced to admit that despite his youthful appearance, despite endless workouts at his exclusive health club back home in Georgetown, despite constant massage and dieting, he was beginning to feel middle-aged. He was tired and would have preferred a cab straight to his destination, but had rather chosen to take a bus, though he abhorred public transport which threw him together with riff-raff like the hairy garlic-smelling fat Italian woman and her ugly brat with whom he had been forced to share a seat.

Remembering her now, he barely suppressed a shudder of disgust. The trouble was, he could not risk a cab because, as he knew from experience, taxi-drivers usually happened to come equipped with inconveniently long memories and the last thing Basil Crimer wanted tonight was a sharp witness who would later recognize him.

He was, after all, supposed to have boarded a flight to Washington several hours earlier. The closest he had come to it was the luggage check-in, after which he had collected his boarding card and promptly made his way out of the airport and back into town. He had also sent a cable to his State Department secretary, saying that due to last minute commitments he had missed his plane and asking that his suitcase be picked up at Washington airport. The telegram was for the benefit of Customs officials, and the secretary would show it to them as proof that he was authorized to retrieve the case. Basil Crimer had every reason to feel smug. He had really thought of everything, even the champagne and the vodka which he had carefully carried tucked under his arm.

Out of the night, a silver BMW appeared and drew up alongside him, flashing its headlights. It stopped, and Crimer got in.

'*Bonsoir, Monsieur Crimer,*' said Gaston Thevet politely.

'*Bonsoir, Monsieur Thevet.*'

'Where to?'

'Just hand me the goods and drive around for a while. Then we'll stop for a drink or two.'

Thevet greedily eyed the bag under Crimer's arm. 'Champagne?'

'The best. And vodka, too.' Thevet's assistant had not lied when Crimer had made a few discreet inquiries in the shop on the Rue du Rhône. Old Gaston really liked his drink.

Thevet started the car, simultaneously handing Crimer a large manila envelope.

Trying to control his impatience, Crimer opened it carefully and extracted three large, beautifully clear photographs of Galina Romanova about to enter what was obviously a hotel room, judging from the number on the door, 504. Basil Crimer knew for a fact that the room in question happened to be Nikolai Golovin's. '*Magnifique*,' he whispered in admiration.

Thevet permitted himself a smile. 'I am glad you like them. You see, you got first choice, as you say.'

'What on earth do you mean?'

'The KGB commissioned me to deliver the same pictures to them, but at the last minute they went back on their deal and refused to pay me the sum we had agreed on. So I was naturally infuriated, *n'est-ce pas*, and so I gave them a set that my photographer carefully blurred as he developed and enlarged them. Clever, huh?' Thevet cackled contentedly. And do you want to know the best part? *C'est vraiment la meilleure* . . . The local KGB man, Glupoff, never thought to check the pictures he got from me. Those photos must be in Moscow by now, and I'm sure that idiot will have a lot of explaining to do, but it's not really his fault, is it? You see, *Monsieur*, those Communist bastards are so mean . . . '

'I couldn't agree more.'

'Do you know what their final offer for the pictures was, Monsieur Crimer? Ten thousand Swiss Francs, including expenses, and we had agreed on fifty thousand. So they get what they deserve.'

'I'll double that. These photographs are absolutely priceless.'

Thevet's eyes shone with pure greed. 'I think this calls for a little celebration, don't you, Monsieur Crimer?'

'Indeed. Why don't you pull up there, by the bridge, and we'll open the vodka and then the champagne.' He indicated the spot he had passed earlier on foot.

'Can you imagine, those Russians falling for my little trick? *Quels imbéciles, n'est-ce pas, Monsieur Crimer?*'

And all of a sudden Gaston Thevet's little round frame was shaking with hysterical laughter.

Crimer joined in with a loud, sincere

belly laugh. He meant it too, for his joke was even funnier, though Thevet did not know it.

Both men were still laughing when Crimer jumped out of the BMW and the chocolatier, with one bottle of vodka and two of champagne inside him, steered his car towards the bridge and plunged headlong into the river Arve.

★   ★   ★

Nikolai Golovin always felt like an excited first-time tourist when he returned to his beloved city after any length of time spent away from it. Now, as the cab drove past the huge esplanade of Red Square, with the gold onion domes of St Basil the Blessed shimmering in the watery winter sun, he once more delighted in the sights of his native town. In his life of wandering all over the world he had never found anything to compare with its sheer size and sweep and grandeur. As the driver turned into the Arbat, the main shopping-street, already busy with early customers eager for supplies, he reflected that

Moscow, like London, was a city that crept outwards, spawning giant suburbs created, in turn, by a chronic housing shortage. Shortages, he knew, had long been the unhappy lot of Soviet citizens. Is life in your country really as miserable as that, Galina had asked, as she listened to Vladimir Vissotsky's satirical ballads. He sighed. Galina was by now a sweet tender memory, Galina who was so vulnerable, such a little girl lost in a world where she wandered like an exile from another, friendlier planet.

Galina was in fact, the exact foil to his wife Natalia, whom he would very soon see. Natalia was very much a part of this world, and not in the least bit lost. He wondered what sort of welcome she reserved for him, or whether she was in at all. It was just a few minutes past noon, and she might well be at the Headquarters of the Culture Commission where she spent her days and, he believed, a good deal of her nights when she was not with one of her many lovers. Strange bedfellows, he and Natalia, engaged in a constant and exhausting power-play, even long-distance. He would spend blissful weeks, even months away from her on foreign assignments, he no longer missed her or yearned to see her, yet he never forgot to buy a bottle of her favourite perfume — 'First' — on the way home. Even on this trip he had been unable to break that tradition. If she was not in, he would leave it on her dresser.

To his surprise, she was in, attired in a gown of flaming red silk, the colour of the *Firebird* she had danced so long ago, and he had to admit that, as usual, she looked stunning. Behind her, he caught a glimpse of the dining-room table laden with all manner of food and drink. She was up to no good, he could tell. After all those years with her, she held little mystery for him.

He put his case down and eyed her coolly. '*Zdrastvuy, Natasha.* You are looking well. Obviously your new duties agree with you.'

She held his glance. 'So do you, Nikolai. You must have had a good time.'

He ignored the sarcasm in her voice. 'I

133

can see you've gone to great pains to prepare lunch.'

'Oh, Marfa helped.' Marfa was their daily, whose miserable fate it was to clean up the mess Natalia left behind. He had to hand it to his wife for true equality with the working-classes.

'Why, Natasha *dorogaya*, it's not like you to be so domestic, not like you at all. Are we expecting guests? A luncheon party for your colleagues on the Culture Commission, perhaps?' he inquired innocently.

'Not at all. Just you and me.'

'*Kak trogatelno*. How very, very touching.'

'*Poidem*.' She took his arm, giving him the uncanny feeling that she considered him as one among the collector's items in her fancy apartment. So be it. She was in for a few surprises, too.

'*S priezdom, Nikolai*.' She raised her vodka glass, then knocked it back, setting it down on the table, empty. 'Welcome home.'

'*Spasibo*. By the way, I have something for you.'

'Really, Nikolai? What is it?' she asked a little too breathlessly, her eyes shining wide and bright and innocent.

He was not taken in by her display of schoolgirlish enthusiasm. He had forgotten how sick she made him when she put on one of her off-stage acts. 'How could I ever have forgotten you, my darling? You are such an exemplary wife,' he answered, parodying her false sweetness.

'As good to you as you are to me, Nikolai.' Her laugh was hard, bitter.

He looked at her coldly. 'Tell me, Natalia, why did you try and get your friend Rudenko to snoop on me in Geneva?'

'You were seeing a woman.'

'That's a good one. You're not exactly virginal yourself are you, my pet.'

'*Khorosho*, Nikolai, you think you can flit from one glamorous assignment to another, building up your career, working on your prospects for the Ambassadorship, which I'm sure you'll get, and leave me behind, content with a phone call once in a while from Geneva or Tokyo or wherever. I've helped you in your career,

I've invited the right people and dragged you to the right parties, so I want a cut of whatever is in store for you. Look, I was not prepared to discuss this . . . '

He slammed his fist down so hard that some of her precious crystal glasses smashed on the floor. 'The reason you don't want to talk about it is that you've been caught at your own game, haven't you, and you don't have a shred of evidence against me.'

She stared at him, open-mouthed. 'How do you know?' she whispered.

'Because Rudenko's local man in Geneva, Oleg Glupoff, is a world-class idiot, who contracted someone to take his damn pictures for him, and then refused to pay what the guy asked. So what you got is worse than useless, right?'

She nodded. Tears began to spill down her cheeks, taking her elaborate stage make-up with them and spreading it over her face in black rivulets. Suddenly she seemed such a ridiculous old hag that he was tempted to laugh.

'Glupoff is, moreover, a coward who quickly caved in under a little friendly persuasion and did not hesitate to spill the beans. I'll spare you the unpleasant details, which might spoil your appetite.' He looked at his wife with such pure disdain that she turned away. Relentlessly, he went on. 'I have already warned you, Natalia, that if you meddle in my life I will make sure that your very interesting past record goes straight to the editor of *Pravda*. And it's a juicy morsel too, isn't it, my pet?' His voice was steely, dangerous.

She began to tremble violently. 'You mean . . . '

'Precisely. Your illegal dealings with the Paris jeweller, when you and your girl-friend Galina Brezhneva filled your pockets with hard currency and your dachas with precious stones for sale to the Nomenklatura. I'm sure you know that a lot of people who got rich fast under Brezhnev are now being hauled before the courts for corruption. I'm sure too that your friend Raisa Maximovna would not like it one bit if her most famous protégée, the star Bolshoi ballerina, were known to have dipped her hand in the cookie jar, as the Americans say. You should have kept your secret, Natalia, and never told me. It's too late now. I can have you put away, if I want to.'

'*Svoloch*,' she hissed, but he slammed the door so violently that the insult was totally lost on him.

10

Geneva, December, 1985

The meeting droned on, as was the wont
of many a United Nations session Galina
had worked for. ' . . . *Y en conclusión,
señor presidente, quisiera una vez mas
rechazar todas aquellas falsas alegaciones
respecto de la violación de los derechos
humanos en Chile. Muchas gracias.*'
Doing her best to keep the sarcasm out of
her voice — an interpreter was, after all,
supposed to be impartial — Galina
faithfully repeated in English ' . . . and in
conclusion, Mr Chairman, allow me once
more to reject any false allegations
regarding human rights violations in
Chile. Thank you.'

'I thank His Excellency, the Ambassador of Chile for his brilliant statement,'
said the representative of Iran, who was
chairing the meeting. 'I am sure we were
all relieved to hear the human rights

situation in his country is improving.'

'Everyone knows that bastard is one of Khomeyny's worst zealots,' commented Galina to her colleague, a very cute young man whose name, Brad Bradley, sounded like a stammer. Brad, whose main concern was his new boyfriend, tugged on his Dior scarf, shifted his slim hips tightly encased in a black leather suit, and crooned, 'Wouldn't worry about it, my dear, happens all the time. It's all a pack of lies, anyhow, and they are all very good at that at the UN.' And he went back to his newspaper.

True, she thought bitterly, true, but it does not make things any better, does it? The Chilean whose statement she had just interpreted had a well-known record as one of Pinochet's most refined torturers, though no one had really been able to prove it, and the Iranian had been a member of the Ayatollah's Revolutionary Guards, walking around with bags of crushed glass destined to disfigure recalcitrant women who refused to wear the tchador. In recognition of his loyal services to the Islamic revolution,

Khomeyny had appointed him Ambassador to the United Nations in Geneva, where he specialized in human rights issues.

She yearned to discuss her feelings with someone who shared them, someone who was not as jaded as Brad Bradley. Nikolai Golovin, for instance, who despite his extensive experience of international meetings, had some idealism, some faith left in the chances for a better world. Nikolai. Since she parted from him, over three weeks ago, she had missed him so achingly as was out of all proportion to their brief time together. The worst of it was that in all likelihood she would never see him again, or if she did, it would be as a colleague, without the slightest hope of resuming their passionate affair. He was probably back in Moscow now, back with his ambitious wife with whom he had a functional marriage, an arrangement that, despite its lovelessness, seemed to work and survive.

'The meeting is adjourned,' she heard the chairman say.

'Oh good, good,' yelped Brad Bradley,

jumping to his feet. 'Have a nice week-end, Galina.' And he was gone, longing no doubt to fall into his boyfriend's arms.

Have a nice week-end. It would be another lonely two days in this bleak December, in this town where she knew no one. Well, in another week or so she would be going home to New York where at least there was theatre and museums and movies which were not dubbed into French, where there was life in the streets after nine o'clock at night. It was nearly nine now, she realized. The meeting had run very late. Making her way through the giant darkened Palais des Nations, the clicking of her heels on the marble floor reverberated hollowly in the shadows of the *Salle des Pas Perdus*, the Hall of the Lost Steps, as it was called. Looking out of the tall windows, she saw that it had begun to snow again. Well, her hotel was not far off, just a couple of blocks down the road on the Rue de Lausanne. She would have a light supper, then go to bed and forget the world.

She was walking briskly towards the

main gate, when the roar of a car engine made her jump hastily out of the way. As the sleek white Mercedes drove slowly past, Galina thought her imagination must have played a trick on her. Kurt von Steuben, the Director General, was at the wheel, and next to him was none other than Basil Crimer, who was supposed to have left for Washington three weeks ago.

★   ★   ★

'Basil, stop your pacing. It's driving me crazy,' snapped Kurt von Steuben. '*Du calme, mon vieux, du calme.*'

Basil Crimer whirled around, facing the Director General, who was lounging in an armchair by the fireplace, with Parsifal, his Alsatian, peacefully asleep at his feet.

'How can I keep calm when I'm sure she saw me,' he answered irritably, 'and she is nothing if not clever, that Romanova bitch, so she's likely to remember.'

'So what if she does? She has no proof, it's her word against yours, and you will soon be highly enough placed at the

United Nations to find more than one way to shut her up should she decide to make trouble for you.'

You bet I will, thought Crimer, by using the late lamented Thevet's incriminating photographs, which in his anxiety he had almost forgotten he possessed. For some reason he could not readily explain, he decided not to mention them to his host. Those pictures were his secret and his secret alone, and he resentfully remembered that there had not been much he had succeeded in keeping from von Steuben. Well, this was one thing he might share with Kurt in his own sweet time, but then again he might not, he decided, feeling a bit like a naughty child rebelling against an authoritarian parent.

'My dear Basil,' continued von Steuben in his most condescending manner, which he knew the other man hated, 'maybe this little incident will teach you to follow my instructions in future. You should have stayed across the border in Ferney, as I told you, and waited for my call. Coming to my office at the Palais des Nations was a damn fool thing to do. It was your good luck my secretaries had left and the only person who actually saw you will never be able to go public with her story. I've looked at her file. She's alone, poor, and she desperately needs her UN job, so a little friendly persuasion will convince her that she should not attempt to be too indiscreet.'

Crimer looked at the other man, wondering if he somehow knew about the photographs. No, how could he? Still, von Steuben often gave him the disquieting impression he could read people's thoughts, that he looked into your very soul. Basil suppressed an involuntary shudder. He knew von Steuben to be evil, and he knew equally well that he was in the man's unrelenting grip and that it was too late to draw back. Von Steuben went on mercilessly. 'You made a very stupid move. Cloak-and-dagger heroics are not your thing, Basil. You should have consulted me before you did anything as gross as murdering Thevet. Moreover, you killed him on a whim, without a shred of evidence that he knew anything about us.'

Crimer lit a cigarette and resumed his pacing. 'I tried to talk to you at the party . . . '

Von Steuben cut him off sharply. 'You really choose your moment, don't you? A reception for the two most publicized world leaders at history's most publicized summit is not what I would call the most private occasion to discuss how we are going to get rid of the Secretary General of the United Nations.'

'So I had to act on my own.'

'You should have waited.'

'For Thevet to blackmail us?'

'How do you know he was going to?'

'Instinct. Feeling.'

'Rubbish. You lost your cool, that's all.'

'You have to admit it was a neat job. The police just recorded the accident of a man who already had a record for drunken driving.'

'True, but that was more luck than judgment. You were very fortunate no one decided to snoop any further. What a fucking comedy. I'm warning you, Basil. Any more stupid moves and I don't know you. After all this careful planning I simply can't afford to have my future jeopardized by an incompetent fool like you. Sometimes I wonder whether I should drop you and find someone else who will help me do the job.'

'Kurt, please, please . . . ' Crimer was genuinely frightened now. 'I promise you I'll do everything you say to the letter, only let me continue working for you. You know how important this is to me . . . '

The Director General smiled. It was good to have this man grovelling at his feet, good to know the extent of his own power over another human being.

There was a knock on the door. '*Entrez,*' barked von Steuben, annoyed at the interruption. Anneliese walked in, carrying a silver tray and wearing her most winsome smile. 'I thought you gentlemen might like some good after-dinner espresso,' she cooed. 'After all, it must be so exhausting to have to discuss business and as I gave the staff the evening off I thought I'd bring the coffee myself.'

'*Danke, Liebling*, you do think of everything, don't you?' Von Steuben blew her a kiss. She was a tremendous asset, this woman, by far the best investment he had ever made. She certainly was an excellent wife, forever making little gestures she knew would please him. As if that were not enough, she was a first-rate associate and partner, always dispensing the right advice and venturing opinions about people and situations which were invariably accurate. He trusted her completely, trusted her instinct and judgment and unbridled ambition comparable only to his own. When he had first hatched his plan for the Secretary-Generalship, he had of course, shared it with her, as he shared everything else. And she had applauded and encouraged him to get to the top. It was, in fact, she who suggested that Leo Anders might encounter a convenient little accident while on official mission to one of the world's many troublespots. Why wait until he really begins to make trouble for you, why let him go public with information he is compiling about your past, she had argued, and that had been enough to convince him. Besides, he would keep his hands clean. Others would do it for him.

Von Steuben waited until Anneliese had left them alone before continuing. Although he trusted her completely, he saw no point in letting her in on the details of their plan before it was ready. For all her intelligence and her cool, she was still a woman and, as such, fundamentally unable to reason logically. This was man's business and it was best to have her completely out of the way while working it out.

He got up, tossed another log into the fireplace, watched the flames wrap around it greedily and take. For a few moments, he stared into the depths of the fire as if it held some coveted secret, then turned to his companion.

'Basil.' Crimer looked at him sharply, startled by the urgency of the tone. 'I want you to listen to me carefully, and to register every word I'm saying. Got it?'

'Go ahead.'

'You will leave from Paris for New York tomorrow afternoon. It's all arranged, so you have nothing to worry about. Just be at Roissy airport at five to pick up your ticket from the Air France counter. Your flight leaves at six-thirty. When you get to New York, you will book into the Pierre Hotel, where a suite has been reserved for you. You will then contact and get to know a certain Brian Crowley.'

'Who the hell's Brian Crowley?'

'A very ambitious, very servile young man who works in the Secretary General's office. The interesting thing about Brian Crowley, as far as we are concerned, is that he is Anders' personal assistant and, in that capacity, he often accompanies the Secretary General on mission.'

'Kurt, you are talking in riddles. I'm afraid I don't follow.'

Von Steuben smiled, a trifle condescendingly. 'Well, I'll spell it out for you. Most, if not all, UN travel involves flying, which in these days of terrorism and sabotage can be a risky business. You know, when a bomb goes off aboard a plane there isn't much of a chance of anyone surviving, is there? Well, young Brian is going to place that bomb on his

150

boss's plane for us.'

'You are not suggesting . . . ?'

'That we tell him he is going on a suicide mission which is going to kill the United Nations Secretary General and his entire entourage, including Brian Crowley? I credit you with more intelligence than that, Basil, but maybe I'm wrong after all.'

Crimer chose to ignore the barb. 'I think I'm entitled to an explanation.'

'By all means, my friend. You see, Brian Crowley has three weaknesses, all of them incurable: his ambition, his stupidity, and his homosexuality. And we shall make use of all three.'

'Just how, if I may know, does all this fit in with your master plan?'

'Very simply . . . You will meet Brian, find a way to appeal to his vanity, which shouldn't be too difficult, then you will become friendly with him and convince him you have the same . . . shall we say, proclivities.'

A look of utter revulsion crossed Crimer's face. 'You surely don't mean . . . '

151

Von Steuben's tone was frosty. 'Yes, if necessary.'

'I couldn't. Never in a million years, Kurt. The whole idea is so disgusting I couldn't go through with it. You can't possibly ask that of me.'

'That's where you are wrong. I'm not asking you, I'm telling you. Of course, you can choose to back out of the whole thing now, but be advised your decision will not be without its consequences. If you dump me, I'll blow your cover, and Thevet's murder will be front-page news.'

Crimer slumped into a chair and put his face in his hands. Von Steuben noticed with pleasure that he was shaking.

'Well, Basil?' he inquired sweetly.

Crimer nodded helplessly.

'Right, I take it you agree with my plan then. As I was saying, you will strike up this nice friendship with Brian Crowley. You will invite him out, lavish all manner of expensive gifts on him. Sooner or later, Brian will introduce you to his circle of close friends. Among them, you will meet one Manuel Mendez.'

'How does he come into all this?'

'Do you remember how a few years ago Fidel Castro fooled the United States Government by unloading a group of so-called 'political exiles' on American shores?'

'Of course I do. They were called the *marielitos*, because they were taken from Mariel harbour to the coast of Florida by US boats, despatched to pick them up.'

'Right. And you also no doubt remember most of them were common criminals, who then spread from Florida all over the United States, so it became virtually impossible for the Department of Justice to track them down. It was Castro's cosmic joke which kept him laughing for quite some time at the expense of the *imperialistas yanquis*.'

Crimer's face lit up. 'And Manuel Mendez is one of them?' he almost shouted, with the eagerness of a schoolboy who knew he had pleased his teacher with the right answer.

'Well done, my friend. You've got it.'

Crimer beamed.

'Manuel Mendez,' continued von Steuben, 'is a very special *marielito*. Back in Havana, drug-peddling was one of his many talents. He was also connected with the Mafia casinos whose closure Castro ordered back in the seventies and for which transgression he almost paid with his life.'

'Pity he didn't.'

'True. I know your views, Basil, and I happen to agree with you wholeheartedly, but that's not the point at issue right now. For his many extra-curricular activities, Manuel Mendez was eventually nailed by the Cuban police and he did some time in Mariel prison. Being one of its toughest inmates, he was released by Castro and shipped to the United States to help poison American society, at which he has proved excellent. He has been success-fully involved with the big-time Mafia in New York, and he has kept some people well supplied with the best heroin money can buy. And Brian Crowley buys. In fact, Manuel Mendez makes sure the habit keeps him good and broke . . . and dependent on the *marielito*'s favours.'

'Get to the point, Kurt.'

'In a minute. I thought you might find

the background interesting and necessary. You see, Manuel Mendez also happens to have connections who deal in illegal guns and explosives. A time bomb is, after all, a very simple device which can be easily concealed.' Von Steuben glanced at his watch. 'And now I think you'd better go. You have an early start tomorrow. Just remember, when all this is over, there will be a very big post waiting for you, no less than right-hand man to Secretary General von Steuben.'

'You seem very sure of being elected.'

Von Steuben grinned, amused. 'And why shouldn't I? I have it on good authority that if my candidature came up, the two states on the Security Council that matter, the United States and the Soviet Union, will give me their unqualified support. After all, I have had a distinguished diplomatic career, particularly in the humanitarian field, and I haven't stepped on anybody's toes. And that, after all, is what counts at the United Nations, isn't it?'

11

New York, April, 1986

'Do you really have to go back to work
now?' asked Bill incredulous.

Galina nodded, twirling the *fettuccine
primavera* around her fork. It was one of
her favourite dishes at Sardi's, the oldest
and most quaint restaurant in New York's
theaterland. They were sitting on a red
plush banquette under rows of photographs of show-business people. A few
tables away, the cast of 'A Chorus Line',
which they had just been to see, were
celebrating yet another night of well-
deserved triumph.

'So what's happening at the United
Nations that requires Miss Galina
Romanova's presence at midnight?' He
could barely contain his sarcasm, for the
simple reason that he had been looking
forward to spending the night with her,
and now his prospects seemed very

much compromised.

'A Security Council debate on the Middle East. Lebanon has requested the meeting, as a result of border skirmishes with Israel. They fear the crisis might escalate again.'

'Can't they wait until tomorrow?'

She put her fork down with a louder clatter than she had intended. 'Look, Bill. I want you to understand something. A sovereign country is not going to await your pleasure, or mine. Do you think the Palestinians and the Israelis will stop their territorial squabbles and call a truce just because you happen to want to make love to me?'

'Oh I happen to want it plenty. Trouble is, since you came back from Geneva, you don't seem to want to.'

Galina did not bother to answer. There was nothing she could say, especially as it was true. Her stay in Geneva seemed to have been a sort of watershed and she had come back truly torn between passion and reality. Nikolai was the passion, the call of the wild, while Bill was the reality, the lure of a stable relationship. In her heart of hearts, Galina knew that she would one day marry her reliable Wall Street stock-broker, and she knew she wanted to. Bill had none of Nikolai's glamour, but at least he loved her more than Nikolai ever would or could. Yes, she would marry him and lead a nice cushy life dividing her time between Manhattan's Upper East Side and his summer house in West Hampton. She would build a family with him to replace the blood family she had lost, and she would be content and secure and loved. And yet, it was so bitterly hard to shed the dream of ecstasy she had shared with Nikolai, so very painful.

Suddenly, she felt sorry for Bill, who sat slumped on the banquette, six feet tall and helpless. 'Bill, listen,' she said gently. 'I don't know what it is, but I can't. There's work, which takes up a lot of my time, and that is something you ought to understand because you have fifteen-hour days.'

'But I'm a man.'

She burst out laughing, which irritated

him no end. 'Work's gone to your head,' he snapped. 'When I met you, you were lost and forlorn and it made me feel good that you needed me so much. And now look at you, the brilliantly successful career woman, the feminist bitch who doesn't need anyone. Well, if you are that independent, you can make your way to the UN on your own, even at midnight. New York streets should not scare you. And while we are at it, you can also pay for the dinner. Go to hell.'

He threw his serviette down, pushed the table back all too forcefully, and left the restaurant. Galina did not attempt to stop him. Maybe it was for the best after all. She signalled to the waiter, who had politely ignored the whole scene — the staff at Sardi's were, after all, used to temperamental stage people — and calmly gathered her belongings. She had exactly twenty minutes to get to the Security Council Chamber.

★   ★   ★

From her booth Galina could see the delegates beginning to take their seats around the horseshoe table while scores of Secretariat staff ran around the room with arms full of documents that the conference officers were shortly to distribute. The press gallery was packed, the television cameras set to roll, the trappings of show business in place. Despite her disillusionment with the world organization, despite the corruption she knew to exist within its walls, she still could not help experiencing a tinge of excitement, mingled with a dose of healthy stage fright, to know that the debate would soon be carried over the air-waves and her voice with it. Her mind darted back to her argument with Bill, who would never in a million years understand that she needed this tension and strain, that the sheer challenge of it all made her come alive and enjoy the passing moments of glamour her job offered.

Behind her, she heard her colleague's heavy footsteps. She half turned to see Gudrun Olafsson walk into the booth, swaying dangerously from side to side. If a mountain could move, thought Galina, it would look like Gudrun Olafsson. Gudrun, whose Viking name and looks did honour to her Norwegian ancestry, had a miserable love life and an inveterate drinking habit, which had caused several unpleasant incidents when she became unable to string a coherent sentence together while interpreting for highly sensitive meetings. And this, realized Galina, sinking into her seat, is going to be one such occasion.

'Evening,' barked Gudrun, falling into her chair, 'what the devil are you doing here?'

'Good evening, Mrs Olafsson,' replied Galina politely. She resolved that she would not be drawn into any arguments, particularly as she had experienced the unpleasantness of the woman's vicious tongue and she could well do without it. She knew, moreover, that since her assignment to the Geneva summit, Gudrun had hated her guts because she had felt upstaged by the snippet of a girl who was so junior to her. Now there was a silent, insidious war of attrition between them, occasionally interspersed with an uneasy truce when they were forced to cohabit in a small glass booth for a few hours.

The meeting was about to begin. The President of the Security Council for that month, a statuesque Senegalese diplomat, walked into the chamber accompanied by Secretary General Anders, who looked as if he badly needed a sleep cure, so strenuous were the demands of his office. Behind Leo Anders, like a Pekinese yapping around the master's feet, came the ultimate in servile civil servants, well-known to Galina and everybody else in the Secretariat as Brian Crowley.

★   ★   ★

Brian was on tenterhooks. Throughout the endless Israeli-Arab debate, he kept harping on the call he had received that morning as he was getting ready to leave for work.

'Mr Crowley?' The man's voice was soft, almost sensuous. A shiver of pleasure ran down Brian's back. 'Mr Brian Crowley?'

'Speaking,' he managed to utter. This sounded interesting, and with his friend Manuel out of town for a few days, Brian Crowley needed some substitute entertainment.

'My name's Robert Bailey. I am a reporter for a new magazine called *Manhattan Profiles* and we are on the lookout for interviews with personalities that shape our New York City life. You know,' the caller's voice grew more confidential, as if he were sharing a secret with an equal, 'interesting, trendy people.'

Brian Crowley swallowed hard. If only his mother back in Salt Lake City could hear this. She had never believed he would really make it in the Big Apple. And here he was, about to be interviewed by a major new magazine. Wow.

'Mr Crowley?' The caller sounded anxious. 'Are you still there?'

'Oh yes, very much so.' It was best to adopt a cool, aloof, but polite tone. He was, after all, sought after, he was a personality and he was doing this reporter a favour, allowing himself to be interviewed. They would all be knocking on his door soon. He would have to take time off to appear on television. He could just see Barbara Walters or Johnny Carson saying, 'Ladies and gentlemen, today we are honoured to have Mr Brian Crowley with us. Mr Crowley is senior assistant to the Secretary General of the United Nations and, despite pressing duties and an extremely crowded schedule, he has kindly agreed to be interviewed today.' Wow. Manuel would be impressed, not to mention the folks back home in Utah.

'How about having a drink at PJ Clarke's?' The reporter's voice startled Brian out of his fantasy.

'Uh?'

'PJ Clarke's. A drink at PJ Clarke's,' repeated the caller slowly, as if talking to an idiot.

Brian Crowley managed to recover his wits. 'Fine. But it will have to be late. There is a United Nations Security Council meeting on the Middle East tonight and . . . '

'I understand you are a very important person, Mr Crowley. Shall we say midnight?'

'I would prefer one a.m., or even two, if that's convenient.' He had to avoid getting old Anders mad by trying to get off early. It was the one thing the boss could not stand, people of less than total devotion to the United Nations, and Brian was desperate for his promotion.

'Two's just fine, Mr Crowley. See you then. By the way, I will not be bringing a tape recorder along, so we can have a free-wheeling, relaxed talk and you can feel comfortable telling me about your-self.'

★   ★   ★

Brian did tell the reporter about himself, at great length. He described his child-hood in Salt Lake City, where he had grown up the youngest of ten children in a Mormon family where to be fruitful and multiply was considered a blessing. So his parents were fruitful and multiplied and his father sang hymns to the Lord in the

Tabernacle choir.

'And I take it you did not fit in?' asked the interviewer.

'Right,' nodded Brian, 'you are quick off the mark.'

Had he not sized up Brian Crowley as a prize idiot, he would have felt flattered. 'So what's a nice boy from Salt Lake City doing in an evil place like New York?' he teased.

Brian's pale eyes shone with excitement. 'This is where it's at, man,' he yelled, to make himself heard over the din at PJ Clarke's, by now jammed with serious and inveterate commuters who had put in such a late day at the office they had missed the ten o'clock back to Westchester and were forced to spend the night in Manhattan on the company expense account. 'Look at all these people,' he continued, 'they are rich, man, very rich. They can have anything they want.'

And you are pathetic, thought his companion, a bumbling fool. Suddenly, he felt almost sorry for Brian Crowley. He pushed pity out of his mind. 'Tell me,

Brian, how did you join the United Nations?'

'Well, I got a law degree from Utah State.' Brian hesitated. He could not possibly tell a magazine writer that he had barely scraped through by the skin of his teeth.

'And?'

'I . . . I had always been looking for wider horizons, so I came to New York, though my family was dead against it.' The truth, he remembered, is that they were delighted to get rid of me after I was picked up for trying to seduce one of the younger members of the Mormon Tabernacle Choir. He felt his forehead moistening when he recalled how glad he had been to go to jail to escape being lynched.

'I do admire your guts, Brian, leaving your hometown and moving here. It must have been desperately lonely for you at first,' he commented with what he hoped was genuine sympathy.

'Oh it was, believe you me. Sometimes, I was sorely tempted to go back home.' That, at least, was the truth. He remembered his stifling room in the transient hotel, the money running out, the meagre job prospects. At least his angry neighbours back in Salt Lake City were familiar, even if they had tried to lynch him. Yes, New York had been a miserable, lonely place. Until the day he met Manuel Mendez in a bar in Greenwich Village. 'Then, one day, I met someone who introduced me to a highly placed diplomat at the United Nations, and the diplomat happened to know the Deputy Director of the Human Rights Division. You know how it is in this life, connections mean everything.' He giggled, pleased with his own equivocation. Manuel, his new lover, was indeed well acquainted with a South American Ambassador to the United Nations, whom he kept well supplied with the purest Colombian cocaine. Manuel then put intolerable pressure on His Excellency, threatening to cut off the flow if Brian Crowley was not hired, and the Ambassador, panic-stricken, paid a hasty visit to the then Secretary General, another Latin

American, whose spinelessness made him perfect for the job. So after a sham interview, Brian Crowley was hired to add to the deadwood Leo Anders inherited when he succeeded the Latin American.

'I heard you have had a brilliant career, Mr Crowley . . . '

'Oh please call me Brian.'

'Brian, you've had a brilliant career and that is why my editors sent me to interview you, because our magazine is geared to the winner. And if you've won in Manhattan, then you've got it made.'

Brian flushed with pleasure. 'You are too kind . . . '

'Believe me, I am not. But I like a winner when I see one, and I like you very much.' His voice became soft caressing, the voice that had first thrilled Brian over the telephone. 'Do you think we could go somewhere . . . quieter?'

Brian swallowed hard. This man, with his distinguished silver hair, his impeccable elegance, his flattery, certainly knew how to turn a guy on. 'Where . . . where would you suggest?'

'Well, why don't you invite me over to your place?'

'I'd love to, Mr Bailey,' whispered Brian hoarsely.

'Please call me Robert,' said Basil Crimer, 'and now, shall we?'

12

'So when are you going to introduce me to your friend Manuel?' asked Basil, trying to keep the irritation out of his voice, which was not easy. Brian seemed to be stalling, stringing him along and, what was worse, plaguing him with ever more insatiable sexual demands.

'I told you, darling, you've got to be patient. We have to wait for Manuel to get in touch. He'll name the time and place. That's the way he usually operates, and he hates being rushed.' With one arm, Brian reached for his cigarettes, while keeping the other stretched over Crimer's naked buttocks. Crimer made an attempt to move away from his lover's touch, edging to the other side of the cavernous bed, but Brian's hold on him tightened immediately, like a predator's. Crimer was

171

unable to repress a shiver of sheer revulsion.

'Cold, darling?' asked Brian solicitously, moving closer to his companion.

'No, not really.'

'But I think you are, sweetheart. Come here and let your Brian warm you up.'

Jesus. Not again. But he had no choice, not if he wanted their plan to go ahead, no choice but to keep Brian Crowley sweet. If he failed now, just short of the ultimate goal, von Steuben would never forgive him. Oh, but he wished he had some news, something to tell Kurt, who must be getting impatient too, by now. Damn it, he simply wished they could talk, have a heart-to-heart. Here he was, stuck in mid-town Manhattan, in this fortieth floor apartment entirely done up in red and black, sharing a bed with a queer sex maniac. What was worse, he had been involved in this situation for two weeks now, it was getting on for the end of May, and no sign of Manuel Mendez. And Kurt had strictly forbidden him to get in touch unless there was some major breakthrough.

As if in a nightmare, he felt Brian Crowley's moist lips on his.

★ ★ ★

Manuel Mendez ordered another drink and looked at his watch. Ten o'clock. The restaurant would soon be closing, and he would be forced to wait out in the street, which was not his idea of fun on Atlantic Avenue in Brooklyn. He had picked this area for no particular reason, except that it was close to the rented room he happened to be staying in this week. He lit a cigarette and sighed heavily. It was no joy, moving from rented room to rented room. *Como un maldito refugiado*, he thought. But he was a goddamn refugee, had been since he left Havana. Even the United States Immigration and Naturalization Service listed him as a refugee, only to those idiots he was a political. Well, Fidel had fooled them all right. He knew that some of his fellow *marielitos* had not done as well as he. At least he, Manuel Mendez, with his velvet black eyes and shapely body, had managed to charm the people who mattered, including some United Nations diplomats. And diplomats meant Customs immunity, which had been a priceless asset to his Colombian drug connection. He was making good money, importing heroin and cocaine from Bogotá via the diplomatic pouch. Of course, his friends at the United Nations got a free cut, but business was business and there was still a lot left to be sold on New York city streets at astronomical prices. Soon, very soon, he would be able to trade this filthy garbage dump they called New York City for a South Sea island of white sand beaches and golden-skinned young boys.

Ten thirty. Where was Diego's chauffeur? To pass the time, he called for the waiter and ordered a couscous, which he recalled was excellent in this Arab restaurant, one of the many that lined Atlantic Avenue. As soon as he had the goods, he would get in touch with Brian Crowley. He could not stand that fool, or the idea of his flabby body or his whining servility. But Brian was one of his best customers and business held no room for personal feelings.

Suddenly his heart jumped. Outside, he could see the familiar limousine with diplomatic plates draw up to the kerb, and a uniformed driver step out and walk towards the restaurant, carrying a crocodile briefcase. The goods had arrived.

★　★　★

The Penal Colony was the most popular gay bar in New York City. Located downtown in the East Village, which had been a disreputable neighbourhood until real-estate developers discovered it in the early eighties, it boasted the best drag show in town, featuring a bevy of young and luscious transvestites. The walls were decorated with studded belts and whips and all manner of S & M paraphernalia, and the air was thick with the smoke of marijuana.

Brian Crowley and Basil Crimer had not come either for the show or for the decor. They had more important business on hand, or at least Crimer did. When they arrived, Manuel was waiting for them, leaning on the bar and nonchalantly sipping a daiquiri. He was, Basil had to admit, gorgeous by any standards, with thick black hair and caramel skin, starkly brought out by the immaculate white leather suit he was wearing.

'Greetings, Brian,' he said raising his glass, 'wha' you gonna have?'

'A whisky sour, please.' Brian's voice was strangely small and tight. 'Straight up.'

'An' you, mister?,' Manuel turned to Crimer.

'This is Bob Bailey, Manuel,' Brian said quickly. 'He's okay.'

Manuel's eyes narrowed as he examined Brian's companion. Crimer squirmed under the Cuban's cold, clinical scrutiny. He was beginning to dislike this whole adventure intensely.

'Yeah, I guess if he's with you, he mus' be okay,' said Manuel, apparently satisfied. 'Will you have a drink, Bob?'

'Double Scotch on the rocks, please.'

Manuel ordered and turned to Brian again. 'Got the bread?' Brian took out a thick envelope and handed it to Mendez, who pocketed it, at the same time placing a box of Lindt chocolates on the countertop. 'Swiss chocolates. The best.'

'Well done, Manuel. We'll have a party Friday night, if you want. My place.'

'Terrific.'

On the floor, the late show was starting. A young man dressed up as Marlene Dietrich was throatily singing a selection from 'The Blue Angel' which Crimer thought an extremely corny and poor imitation of 'Cabaret'. In fact, had the whole situation not been so deadly serious, he would have been tempted to laugh outright.

Manuel's eyes glazed over. He was clearly bored to utter distraction by the performance. A sign of intelligence, thought Crimer. Bodes well for the job we have in mind for him. He had to admit Kurt von Steuben had certainly made the right contacts. Manuel Mendez did seem to be an efficient killing-machine, and that was precisely what they needed. And Brian Crowley, he could now see, would make the perfect pawn to carry out the plan without a hitch.

Somehow, he had to talk to Manuel alone, and the sooner the better.

Brian seemed absorbed in the floor show. Knowing it was risky, but eager to get it over and done with, Crimer dropped his voice and whispered in Manuel's ear, 'Could we meet someplace?'

The Cuban stared straight ahead, as if he had not heard. Basil went cold inside. He was being completely ignored.

He tried again. 'Manuel . . . '

'Yeah, I heard ya the first time.'

Silence. Crimer summoned his courage. 'And what do you say?'

'Shh,' snapped Brian indignantly, 'if you two want to talk . . . '

Manuel ignored him too. 'All right,' he whispered back to Crimer. 'But it better be good. An' I don' like no dirty tricks, understan'?'

Crimer nodded. 'Sure I do, man.'

'Will you be at Brian's party?'

'Sure.'

'We'll talk then.'

'Look here,' yelped Brian, 'I told you that if you don't shut up . . . ' He wagged an admonishing finger. What a relief he's soon going to be dead, thought Crimer, that will make one idiot less in this world.

★ ★ ★

'Wha's in it for me?' asked Manuel.

'A lot of money, if you deliver. You can retire on that.'

The Cuban smiled, savouring the thought. He leaned back in his chair and his eyes feasted on New York by night. They were dining at the Windows on the World restaurant on the one-hundred-and-fourth floor of the World Trade Center. They had managed to slip away from Brian Crowley's party, which by the time they left had turned into a veritable orgy, with the guests either stoned or drunk or making it, or all three, so no one noticed their absence.

'Wha' makes you think I got connections?'

'Well, don't you?'

'*Puede ser*. Maybe.'

'I've been led to believe you do.'

'Wha'?'

That was clearly too difficult. Crimer tried again. 'I've been told you have.'

Manuel smiled. '*Bueno*. Never mind. But you pay in advance.'

'Half on delivery, the other half when it's done.'

'You drive a tough bargain, man.'

'So do you. I don't call half a million dollars cheap.'

'There's a lot involved,' replied Manuel evenly. Crimer eyed him with genuine admiration of his cool versatility. Why, the man was an accomplished actor — in his dark suit and horn-rimmed glasses, he looked more like a staid, respectable Wall Street businessman than a felon contracting to deliver a bomb.

'When you wan' the goods?' asked Manuel politely, pouring himself some more Armagnac.

'I'll let you know.' He prayed Anders would soon be announcing another peace mission. 'Where can I get in touch with you?'

'I'll be contacting you. And now I gotta be going. Thanks for the dinner, man.'

Basil Crimer briefly wondered whether

he would ever see the Cuban again, or whether next thing he knew he would find himself behind bars. He forced the thought out of his mind. He had no choice but to trust Manuel Mendez.

13

For the second time in less than a year, Galina found herself sitting in Leo Anders' office, wondering where the boss would be sending her this time. When Donna had conveyed the Secretary General's summons in suitably solemn tones earlier that morning, Galina felt a strange sense of foreboding, a tightening in the pit of her stomach she could not explain. On the way up to the thirty-eighth floor, she decided that it was the memory of that whole Geneva summit, of her disastrous encounter with Crimer and her bitter affair with Nikolai that made her so nervous.

On the way into Anders' office, she had passed a very flustered Brian Crowley who, true to his officious self, gave her a curt condescending nod — in his estimation, she was too much of an underling to merit a smile. He is probably wondering what I'm doing in these exalted heights, she concluded rightly. He considered her an intruder, and he did not like intruders in what he felt was his territory as Personal Assistant to the Secretary General.

Anders greeted her with his usual courtesy, half-rising in his seat when she came in. 'Good morning, Miss Romanova,' he said warmly, 'how very nice to see you again. Please sit down.'

Galina obliged. 'Good morning, Mr Secretary General. The pleasure is mine,' she answered sincerely.

Anders put his elbows on his desk, made a steeple with his hands and gazed at her for a long moment. He looks tired, thought Galina, I really don't envy him his job. Two years into his tenure, which lasted five, Leo Anders was the target of acrimonious criticism from a good many Member States, especially the most repressive among them, for his coura-geous, independent stance on human rights issues. He was doing something unheard of in the annals of the hypocritical bureaucracy of the United Nations — he was making waves in the calm seas of diplomatic torpor, he was rapping governments over the knuckles for their shoddy record of torture and imprisonment of political dissidents. And he was doing so publicly. Many, drawing the inevitable parallel with Dag Hammarskjöld, predicted that, sooner or later, Leo Anders would pay and pay dearly, maybe even with his life, and Leo Anders happened to agree with them. But he could not have cared less about the risks he was incurring. There were other, higher issues at stake.

'What do you know about Nicaragua, Miss Romanova?' he asked out of the blue.

She shrugged. 'Nothing much, except what you read in the press about the United States-supported Contras fighting the Marxist Sandinista government of President Daniel Ortega.'

'Well, you will soon have the opportunity of finding out a bit more.'

Galina's mouth dropped open. For a moment, she gaped at him like an idiot, then found her voice. 'You are not . . . you are not thinking of sending me on another special mission, are you, Mr Anders?'

Anders laughed, genuinely amused. 'Yes, well, I heard that in Geneva you had some . . . er . . . interpersonal problems with Mr Crimer. But he's known to be difficult, and I think you handled things very well. I have also heard glowing reports about your work at the summit. Both the Soviet and American delegations were very pleased.'

She smiled at the sheer pleasure of her triumph over Basil Crimer. If only he could hear this.

'Well, I have been told that your Spanish is as good as your Russian, you see, and I need an interpreter who can work both ways, Spanish — English and English — Spanish to cover an assignment in Nicaragua in September.'

'When would I be leaving?'

'We will be leaving some time in late September, about one week into the General Assembly session.'

'We?'

'That's right. You will be my personal

interpreter on this mission. I have been officially approached by the Ambassador of Nicaragua to the United Nations with a message from President Ortega, who would like me to go to Managua to draw up a report on allegations of Contra atrocities. The President himself is planning to attend the General Assembly and to issue a public invitation to me from the plenary rostrum.' He paused and looked at her kindly. 'Any questions?'

'Not for the moment, Mr Secretary General.'

'Fine, I'll let you know about the pre-mission briefing, then.'

He was politely asking her to leave. She rose, and he with her. 'Thank you, Mr Anders. I am deeply flattered by your confidence in me.'

'You deserve it, Miss Romanova. Good day.'

On her way out, she glanced at the armchair that next to hers that had remained empty and the memory of Nikolai tugged at her heart with an intensity she had not thought possible after all these months.

Moscow, July 1986

Nikolai Golovin was ushered into Eduard Shevardnadze's private office at the Soviet Ministry for Foreign Affairs by a junior aide who looked like a cherub and behaved like a scared schoolboy.

The Foreign Minister met his guest halfway through the room with arms outstretched and a broad smile on his handsome Georgian face. *'Zdrastvuyte, Nikolai Sergeevich, kak pryatno.* Come in, come in, I'm so very pleased to see you. How's your beautiful wife?'

'Ochen khorosho, spasibo, Eduard Ambrosievich. Ochen zanyata. Very busy indeed with her work on the Cultural Commission. Right now, she's involved in setting up this joint US-USSR Festival called 'Making Music Together' scheduled to take place in Boston some time next year.'

'Well, I'm so glad to tell you she'll be able to work right there, on the spot.'

Nikolai stared at his boss. As if in a trance, he heard the Foreign Minister saying, 'The Central Committee has approved my recommendation for your appointment as our Permanent Representative to United Nations Headquarters in New York. Like me, they feel that your vast experience of the West, your first-rate knowledge of English and French and your intelligent support of Gorbachev's *glasnost* and *perestroika* make you ideal for the job. Not to mention your social graces and your sense of humour, of course.' Shevardnadze winked broadly, and both men laughed. 'This calls for a celebration,' added the Foreign Minister. He opened a cupboard and produced a bottle of wine. 'I just got this red from my family in Tbilisi.' He filled two glasses and handed one to Nikolai. 'It's vintage, fit for the occasion. *Pozdravlayu vas, Tovarisch Posol.*'

'*Spasibo, Tovarisch Ministr.*' Natalia would be ecstatic. He smiled in anticipation of her pleasure. They were getting on reasonably well lately.

New York, early August, 1986

Basil Crimer stood in a filthy phone booth on Times Square, reading the obscene graffiti that almost obliterated the windows and wondering when Manuel would call. Outside, three punks with hair ranging from grass-green to blood-red were beginning to make rude faces and flex the very obvious muscles that bulged through their torn denims. Crimer mopped his brow, wet as much from fear as from the New York summer heat. He figured the temperature had to be in the nineties, with at least as high a percentage of humidity. The air was as still and cloying as molasses.

One of the punks knocked on the window and signalled for Crimer to get out. Christ, if he didn't they would be dragging him out bleeding in a few minutes, under the neons of Times Square. Somehow, he had to weather this, had to wait for Manuel's call. As soon as Brian Crowley had told him about Leo Anders' impending mission to Nicaragua, he had rushed out and phoned Manuel at

The Penal Colony, his home base. When Manuel phoned in, he left the number of the booth on Forty-fourth Street and Broadway, with instructions for Crimer to be there at ten o'clock that evening.

He nearly yanked the receiver out of its socket the minute the phone rang. 'Be at the Reservoir, Central Park,' said Manuel without any preliminaries, 'three o'clock sharp.'

Geneva, mid-August, 1986

Anneliese von Steuben stretched lazily on her deckchair, put down the latest Judith Krantz bestseller she had been trying to read for the past half hour and, with a sigh of supreme contentment, resigned herself to total idleness. From where she was sitting under her parasol, she could see her husband swimming his usual fifty laps in the pool, which, together with his jogging and horse-riding, kept him in trim. She worked out, too, vowing to stay in shape if it killed her. Stay in shape she did, as the mirror had so truthfully told her that morning. Good. She wanted Kurt to be proud of her, wanted to be worthy of him. She liked to think of her marriage as a success, a going concern.

She closed her eyes and opened them again, startled, when she felt her husband's lips on hers. 'You look so delicious, sweetheart. I'd like to make love to you here and now.'

Anneliese glanced furtively over her shoulder, giggling like a schoolgirl at the anticipation of forbidden pleasures. 'And why ever not?' she teased. The staff were under strict instructions not to disturb her this weekend, which she had planned as a treat for herself and her husband. 'No parties, no receptions. Just you and me,' she had said to Kurt earlier in the week. 'It's ages since we've been able to get away from official business.'

'I agree, darling, and if everything goes according to plan, it will be ages again.'

He bent over her and undid the straps of her bathing-suit to expose her breasts. His tongue touched her nipple and she moaned softly.

At that precise moment, the poolside phone purred. Von Steuben swore and picked it up. 'Hello. Yes, I can hear you,' he yelled, turning away from a furious Anneliese, who was busy doing up the straps he had untied just a few blissful minutes ago. 'It's Crimer in New York,' he told his wife's back. 'He's got news.'

She forgot her anger and turned to face him.

'When? In September? Splendid, Basil, couldn't be better. Now listen to me. Just do what you have to do and don't get in touch with me until it's all over. No, of course I am not mad. I do appreciate your calling. Good, good. Yes, you know that, for the moment, I want to keep a low profile.'

He replaced the receiver and turned to Anneliese. 'You have to start thinking about packing, darling. Late September — early October at the very outside — we'll be heading for New York.'

New York, mid-August, 1986

Something was wrong. Manuel had said three o'clock and it was now past three-thirty. In all their dealings so far, Crimer had never known the Cuban to be late and it was now questionable whether he would be turning up at all. Crimer, who had been sitting on a bench by the artificial lake called the Reservoir in Central Park, was hot and tired and not a little worried. Around him, couples embraced and children played and nannies wheeled rich Fifth Avenue babies in fancy prams. All that sweet normalcy was killing him, the more so, he now realized with a stab of regret, because he had a secret hankering for it. In fact, all his underhand manoeuvring and dirty dealing stemmed from a foreigner's desire to belong, to be part of the establishment, a desire that had somehow turned into hatred and greed. He hated the Soviet Union and what it stood for and he had loathed Galina Romanova for associating with a Soviet, detested her for betraying their common heritage of

Russian nobility. That was why his mouth watered at the idea of destroying her, which he would of course do, especially thanks to the incriminating photographs so obligingly supplied by the hapless Gaston Thevet.

Funny, he had not thought of Thevet for days and, even now, he could not say that the murder especially plagued his conscience. It had all turned out to be amazingly easy to kill the stupid little *chocolatier*, far easier than he would have thought.

Now Anders was different. That could not be thought of as a murder either, but rather as an unavoidable political and personal necessity. Political, because the Secretary General had an odd knack for singling out rightist Governments to turn them into public whipping-boys for human rights abuses. In other words, the man was a goddamn Commie, probably in the secret pay of the Soviets, who were gaining increasing ground at the United Nations — you only had to look at the recent spate of appointments of Soviet nationals to high professional posts in the

Secretariat. The Secretary General's death had also become an urgent personal necessity since he had started delving into Kurt von Steuben's past. So what if the man had been a Nazi — in fact, thought Crimer, if there were more of them left the world would be a better place, rid of vermin like Jews and Blacks and the like. Oh yes, Anders had to die and von Steuben had to succeed him and he, Basil Crimer, would be there reaping his just rewards for his loyal, unflinching support. It all made beautiful, perfect sense.

Four o'clock. Where was that Cuban? Probably skipped town with his first instalment. Christ, he should have known better than to trust that refugee riff-raff. That snivelling queer Brian Crowley certainly picked his friends. He would have to phone Kurt back and tell him there had been a hitch. And just as everything was going so well too. He would have to find another solution, but what?

He rose from his bench and was moving towards the exit from the park, when he spotted Manuel walking briskly towards him. The Cuban seemed to have lost all of his usual cool nonchalance. He looked flustered and out of breath, and as he drew closer, Crimer could see his eyes were wide and staring, as if he had just been snorting coke or shooting up. Crimer stopped, but Manuel kept moving without any sign of recognition and when they finally came level, the Cuban whispered, 'Jus' keep walkin', man. I think them cops is followin' me. I'm gettin' outta town for a while.'

As he disappeared down the path, Crimer could see two uniformed New York City policemen entering the park.

14

New York, mid-August, 1986

'I don't understand you, I really don't, Galina. I call you, you agree to see me, then I think things are all right between us again.'

'Look, Bill, it's not a question of 'right' or 'not right'. It's just that I'm trying to juggle two basically incompatible roles. I realize that what you need is not a career woman like me, what you need is a perfect housewife and hostess who will live with you in suburbia like Westchester, entertain your business friends and spend her days ferrying your kids to school in the station-waggon and her evenings playing bridge. But there's just one small hitch that happens to mar your neat little scenario — I happen to love my career, I fully intend to go on working after we're married, so don't even begin to expect me to give it up. Also, may I remind you in passing that it was you who walked out on me last time we met, remember? You left me high and dry to pay the check at Sardi's.'

'I can see you've never forgiven me for it.'

'No, I haven't.'

'What was I to do, Galina? You left me no choice. You were hell-bent on going back to work and . . . '

'It's my job, damn it. How would you feel if I pouted because you have to spend your days on the bloody Stock Exchange floor yelling yourself hoarse along with a bunch of greedy nuts much like yourself?'

'Thank you very much.' Angrily, he crumpled his sandwich wrapper and turned away from her to stare fixedly at the lunch-time crowd of office people who, like them, were taking their break on the esplanade of the new midtown business center called Citicorp. The place was a favourite with yuppies like Bill, maybe, thought Galina, because it was as glossy and as superficial as their life. Nikolai would have hated the whole scene. Nikolai, creeping into her thoughts for the millionth time since Geneva. Angrily, she tried to force him out of her mind, but he refused to budge. Damn. The memory of Nikolai was spoiling her life and the irony of it was that he had probably wiped her clean off his existence by now.

Bill turned to her again, attempting a smile which did not quite come off. 'Look, Galina, I've tried to reason with you, to explain *ad nauseam* that I take a very dim view of my girlfriend rushing off to do midnight work, then meeting me and announcing she's going off on some sort of highly confidential mission in October . . . '

'Two points, Bill. First of all, I am bound by professional secrecy and, as such, not at liberty to reveal the nature of certain assignments. Then, because of the type of work I do and which you claim to understand, you know that I'm supposed to be at the Secretary General's disposal twenty-four hours out of twenty-four. It's in the United Nations Charter and it's spelled out in my contract. If I refuse an assignment I'm acting in direct breach of that contract, which I have no wish to do.'

'Why can't you stay home and have babies like everybody else?' he asked irrelevantly.

'I will, one day. But not yet. For the moment, babies bore me.'

'Sure. Your Commie friends at the United Nations are far more fun.'

She froze, staring at him fixedly. He could not possibly have known about Nikolai.

'Well it's true, isn't it? Everybody knows the United Nations is full of Commies and fellow-travellers like you. That's why some right-thinking members of Congress want to cut down on our contribution to the UN. And I, for one, agree with them. I don't see why we should finance the KGB.'

'I just can't believe what I'm hearing, Bill. It's the first time I've heard you spouting such arrant nonsense.'

'Well, you've driven me to it . . . ' his voice trailed away into a helpless whisper.

She stood up. 'I think I'd better go now,' she said wearily.

He did not bother to answer.

* * *

Galina did not have a meeting that afternoon, so she whiled it away wandering aimlessly around Manhattan. The heat and the pollution were oppressive and, as so often since her parents' death, she felt New York depressed her more and more. For one, it had become much too expensive and, even though she was by no means extravagant, she seemed to be perpetually broke. It was also too overwhelming, too tiring and there were times when she ardently wished she could drop everything, buy a little beach house and spend the remainder of her days listening to sea waves instead of police sirens roaring up First Avenue.

Her feeling of alienation and apartness had strangely deepened since her affair with Nikolai, with whom she had shared an extraordinary closeness, just tasting enough of it to long for more as it was snatched away. So often, she had thought of writing to him, she had begun letters in her mind, only to drop them. What was the use? He had probably forgotten her by now and, even if he had not, he would never answer, of that she was sure. He was, after all, wholly devoted to his country and his career and, why not, to his own self-advancement — he had made that quite plain back in Geneva. He had been monstrously selfish, too, foisting himself on her aware as he was that he was going to hurt her. And she had been the willing, consenting sacrificial lamb. How dramatic. How very banal.

Somehow, she found herself standing in front of the Russian Orthodox Church on Park Avenue and Ninety-fifth Street. Had she meant to come here, or had her steps just brought her to this place naturally, because that is where she wanted to be? It was Thursday night and she remembered there was an evening service and walked in. Inside, in the half-darkness redolent with incense, she glimpsed the gilded Byzantine icons and heard the black-clad priest chanting the ancient Slavonic melody that her father used to love, especially at Easter. She stood there and thought of the onion-domed churches of Russia and wondered whether Nikolai had ever heard that sublime singing which had been part of her childhood and which she still loved so much.

Moscow, mid-August, 1986

'Congratulations, Comrade Ambassador.' Natalia Golovin raised her glass to her husband. '*Pozdravliayu.* Well done.'

Nikolai looked at her, thinking how efficient yet feminine she looked in her strict business suit, with her hair pulled back the way she had worn it since her days as a Bolshoi ballerina. A stack of heavily pencilled programmes and schedules were lying next to her on the table.

'*Spasibo, dorogaya,*' he answered with a slight touch of irony. 'Of course, you'll be reaping the spoils of my new appointment, *Madame l'Ambassadrice.*'

She beamed broadly. 'Naturally. We are partners, aren't we?'

He sighed and lit a cigarette. What was there to say? Yes, they were partners, and since his return from Geneva, since that row they had had when he first came back, they had somehow understood that they still needed each other, that their careers and their unbridled ambition welded them together. Love had not returned, but their marriage had once again become a going concern.

'There's something to be said for private enterprise, isn't there?' she commented, fingering the linen tablecloth, which, like the fresh flowers on the table and fresh produce on the menu, could be found only in new co-operative cafés like the establishment the Golovins happened to be lunching in. 'I guess limited State participation means competition, and competition means pleasing the customers with little frills like air-conditioning, which is a relief. I wish we had similar facilities at the Cultural Commission.'

'How is your work going?' asked Nikolai politely, without interest.

'Oh, just fine. While waiting for you, I've been working on these.' She pointed to the programmes next to her. 'Combined schedules for the Kirov, the American Ballet Theater, the New York City Ballet. What a lot of organizing all this involves, you have no idea.'

'Oh, I'm sure you are doing very well. By the way, a piece of news that will gladden your heart. Rudenko's been replaced. There's talk of a trial on charges of embezzlement.'

'Oh really?' Her eyes opened wide.

What a consummate actress she is, he thought with a mixture of disgust and amusement. He had heard rumours that she had had a hand in the removal of the Deputy Chief of the KGB and, knowing her as he did, he was fairly certain that the rumours had more than a grain of truth to them.

Memories of Galina sprang unbidden into his mind. How different the two women were, he thought, looking at his wife sadly. While Natalia was an accomplished liar, Galina was honest, guileless, incapable of play acting, and that was why it had been so refreshing to be with her. He experienced an overwhelming desire to see her again and, angrily, fought to dismiss it — she was, after all, no part of his life.

New York, late August, 1986

How he managed to survive that month of August, Basil Crimer would never know. Time had slowed down to a virtual crawl, before stopping altogether. Often, as he sat in a cinema watching a film that did not interest him in the least, or drank himself into oblivion in one of the East Side bars, he would glance at his watch, only to realize that it was just five minutes since he had last looked. As he sat downing Scotch upon Scotch, women would approach him, trying to pick him up, but he always discouraged them because for the first time in his adult life, he felt unsure of his sexual prowess. The slow sleepless nights, filled with nothing except Brian Crowley's insatiable amorous advances, had sapped his morale. Trouble was, he had to keep Brian sweet while waiting for something to happen. Von Steuben had advised him to lie low but to keep stoking the fire, so to speak. At least until they heard from Manuel and Leo Anders formulated some definite travel plans.

It was fine for Kurt, thought Crimer resentfully, shooting out orders from his fancy estate in Cologny while he had to sit it out in New York in August. Aside from everything else, he had had to phone the State Department and extend his leave on a flimsy pretext which he was certain his superiors had seen through, and the last thing he wanted was to have his job jeopardized. Lately, La Donnia had been threatening to remarry and cut off his allowance — she had met some rich oil stud from Texas who evidently satisfied her sexual greed, so she had no further need of Basil.

Towards the end of the month, he had reached such a state of depression that he could no longer sleep or wake up without pills, aware as he was that pills and alcohol made a very bad combination.

'What's the matter, darling?' asked Brian solicitously over breakfast one morning. 'You look totally shagged. Bags under your eyes and all. And you are not eating anything. You wouldn't be in love by any chance, would you?' And he winked broadly.

God. How he hated Brian Crowley. He could have murdered him with his bare hands right there and then, in that crazy black and red kitchen of his. With a supreme effort, he held himself in check, reminding himself that the idiot queer would soon be rotting in his grave anyway.

'It's all right, Brian, it's nothing. Probably a touch of the flu.'

'Oh sweetheart, do you want me to stay home and take care of you?'

'No!' yelled Crimer.

'Oh, I'm sorry,' said Brian, pouting.

'No, I'm sorry, Brian. I shouldn't have yelled at you.'

'It's all right, I understand. You don't feel well. Go to bed, drink plenty of liquids and I'll call you later from the office. Old Anders is all het up about his Nicaragua mission sometime in October, so I have to work overtime, I expect. He's terribly demanding. Doesn't pass up one.'

'Oh really?'

'Yes, well I shouldn't really be talking about this especially to a journalist, because it's strictly confidential and I'll be sacked if the Secretary General finds out I've spilled the beans.'

'He won't,' Crimer reassured him.

'Well, I know that, Bob, because I've learnt to trust you. In fact, I trusted you from the first.'

The more fool you, thought Crimer.

Brian took a deep breath, then continued. 'I'll tell you this much. He's expecting an invitation from President Ortega to be issued any minute. Apparently Ortega is thinking of asking him to go to Nicaragua some time in late September. Of course I'll be going with him, I'm his right arm,' he finished with characteristic modesty. 'Will you miss me?'

'Oh, very much,' mumbled his companion. 'Very much indeed, Brian.'

★ ★ ★

Brian told him he would be working late, so he decided to have a night on the town. It turned out to be a bit of a washout, consisting as it did of a mediocre musical on Broadway, a tasteless, pseudo-Italian meal of *lasagne* that tasted and felt like a ton of bricks, and a call-girl who was way over the hill and totally unable to arouse him. More depressed than ever, he made his way back to the apartment. Now that he had priceless information about Anders' forthcoming plans, he could not act on it, and the thought drove him mad with frustration.

Mechanically, he turned the key in the lock and let himself in. The place was in total darkness, and he groped for the light-switch on the wall next to the door.

He could not believe his eyes. There, on the living-room sofa smiling pleasantly at him, was Manuel Mendez.

15

'Hi, man,' said Manuel coolly. 'Help yourself to a drink,' he added gesturing towards Brian's well-stocked liquor cabinet.

'You've got a nerve, you know,' was all Crimer could think of.

Manuel shrugged and drained his glass. 'Gotta take it where you find it, man.'

'Where have you been all this time?' Crimer did not know whether to laugh or cry.

'Oh, here and there. Had to skip town. That day in Central Park, back in July, them cops was on my tracks, so as soon as I lost them, I goes to Port Authority Bus Terminal, see, and gets a ticket to Chicago. Got some friends there. Then I travels around a bit. And now I'm back. You has a contract with me, right.'

'Right.'

'Still innerested?'

'Very much so, yes.'

'When you wants delivery?'

'I don't know exactly yet. As I told you before, late September, I think. I've got to have the dates of his departure confirmed. By the way, Brian told me he will be accompanying the boss for sure.'

Manuel smiled. 'Too bad for poor Brian, eh?'

'Yes, considering the stupid fool will be taking the goods on board himself. Never mind that now. Will you be around for a while?'

'Yeah.'

'Where can I get in touch with you?'

'You got it wrong, mister. I'll be in touch with you.'

'Manuel, I don't want to lose sight of you again.'

'Don't worry, I'll stick around. After all, I wants the money, don't I? When your man flies to Managua, I'll be there already to complete the operation on the ground. After that, I retreat to an island some place, a beautiful island with a beach an' beautiful boys, as far away from this fuckin' country as I can. Adios America. An' now I better go before our Brian gets home an' finds me here with you. He is gonna be jealous, I think.'

Before Crimer could say any more, Manuel Mendez was gone.

New York, late September, 1986

Security was extra-tight at United Nations Headquarters on that Tuesday, September 23rd, the official opening day for the forty-second General Assembly. The session, which lasts three months, is usually inaugurated with a great deal of pomp and circumstance and massive press coverage of visiting Heads of State, Foreign Ministers and assorted dignitaries. For the first few weeks of the Assembly, these personages gather in New York to deliver policy statements in what is mistakenly known as a general debate, for rather than a debate it is an endless stream of monologues for domestic consumption back in the Member States.

This year was no exception, decided Galina as she handed her pass to the guard on duty at the gate. It was a lovely late September day, a relief after the hot torpor of an August which had seemed to drag by more than usual, with all her friends out of town and her relationship with Bill moving from argument to tedious argument. It was a relief to see everything springing back to life after the summer lull.

'What's going on?' she asked the guard on duty. 'The place is like a goddamn fortress.'

The guard looked at her as if she had just come down from the moon. 'You mean you don't know, lady? President Daniel Ortega of Nicaragua is coming to speak today.'

So there it was. Her immediate fate would be decided after this meeting. Anders would probably call her in later today or early tomorrow to brief her about the trip to Managua. Knowing him, he would probably want to get the arrangements for the mission settled as soon as possible. She walked into the building, her heart thundering against her ribs — whether from excitement or nervousness, she could not tell.

Security guards, journalists and curious staff were milling around the lobby, eager for a glimpse of the young Sandinista President whose constant conflict with the United States over the American-funded Contra movement was never out of the papers. Pushing past the small crowd, Galina rode up to the third floor, then walked the length of the corridor to the General Assembly Hall. She pushed a small metal door marked 'Interpreters only,' and found herself in the area housing the glass booths, which were so angled over the vast conference room underneath that they always reminded her of the viewing gallery of an operating theatre.

Her colleague for that morning, David Gold, was already in the booth, reading the New York Times. God forbid he should ever be caught looking at a conference document, thought Galina, it would be beneath his dignity to appear to be making an effort. In a sense, though, she had to admit that after twenty-five years of interpreting for the Organization, he did know everything there was to be known about the many subjects discussed at the United Nations, and that he was outstanding at his job. And he knew it, too.

'Morning,' said David. 'I think you have your work cut out for you.' He pointed to a thick sheaf of paper lying on Galina's side of the booth. 'Conference officer just brought it. It's Ortega's statement, about thirty pages. Well, good luck to you. I suppose you'll be the star of the show again,' he added, with not a little jealousy. Unlike Galina, who interpreted from Russian, Spanish and French, David Gold worked only from Russian and French, so any statements in Spanish were for her to do. She knew that he could not stand being upstaged, especially by a woman and especially when her voice would be going out over radio and television and excerpts from her interpretation would be quoted in all the major English-language newspapers around the world. Trying not to think of her awesome responsibility and not succeeding, she began to prepare the speech.

She was midway through the statement when the President of the General Assembly, the Ambassador of India, graveled the meeting to order. 'I declare open the first meeting of the Forty-second session of the United Nations General Assembly,' he boomed into the microphone. 'I request distinguished delegates to remain seated while the Chief of Protocol escorts His Excellency President Daniel Ortega of Nicaragua and the Secretary General into the Hall.'

Preceded by a flurry of security guards, President Ortega, a small man in battle fatigues, and Secretary General Anders walked down the aisle to the rostrum. The Secretary General took his seat next to the President of the General Assembly, while Daniel Ortega moved up to the rostrum to deliver his statement.

'*Señor Presidente, Señor Secretario General, Excelencias, señors y señores* . . . ,' he began.

Galina switched her microphone on.

For the next hour, President Ortega reviewed the situation of his country and the world, delivered himself of a violent diatribe against the United States for financing, aiding and abetting counter-revolution against the legally constituted Sandinista Government and generally indulged in the Latin love of words and flowery turns of phrase, which Galina did her best to put into elegant English without sounding ridiculous.

'In conclusion,' he said, turning towards the rostrum and looking straight at Leo Anders, 'I should like to issue an invitation to the Secretary General of the United Nations to come to my country as soon as possible. *El propósito de esta visita*,' he went on, 'the purpose of your visit, Mr Secretary General, will be to ascertain for yourself the devastation sown by the counter-revolutionary Contra troops, devastation which is particularly criminal now, at this time in the history of our country, when we are doing our best to rebuild our nation after years of Anastasio Somoza's corrupt rule. *Venga, Señor Secretario General*,' he ended with a flourish. 'Come and see for yourself, come and witness the heroic effort of the people of Nicaragua, a people with a glorious past and working towards an equally glorious future of freedom and prosperity.'

Thunderous applause drowned out the last words of President Ortega's speech and he remained at the rostrum for a few minutes, basking in his popularity, acknowledging it with his arms raised in salute. From where Galina was sitting, she could see the United States delegation rising and walking out of the hall in glum silence. A little further up, already out of her range of vision, the American Ambassador, passing the seat of the USSR delegation, inclined his head politely to his new Soviet counterpart, Nikolai Golovin.

* * *

As Galina had expected, a few hours after the meeting, Leo Anders called her in for a pre-mission briefing. When she arrived in his office, she found him surrounded by a host of aides, including the inevitable Brian Crowley, who, as usual, hovered around his boss like a bumblebee.

The Secretary General acknowledged Galina's presence with a tight little smile, so unlike the relaxed greeting she was used to from him. She was sorry to see he looked tired and tense, no doubt over the forthcoming Nicaragua trip. Presumably, he was having to cross swords with the United States Government, and it was no mean challenge to defy a superpower with veto power on the Security Council and, what was more, the major financial contributor to the United Nations budget. Leo Anders knew full well that, if he crossed the Americans politically, they would refuse to pay, and their refusal would mean sinking the Organization. And yet, he had no choice but to accept President Ortega's invitation, if he was to preserve the independence of his high office.

'Please be seated, everyone.' He waited a few minutes and when he was sure he had his staff's attention, he continued. 'I'll try to keep this as short as possible.

I've called you in to tell you basically two things — you will be flying with me to Managua on October 16th. I can't tell you exactly how long we'll be staying in Nicaragua, though I anticipate it will probably be around a week. The second point is that it will not be an easy mission. We'll be travelling inland, away from the capital, to interview Sandinista troops and Contra leaders. Often, we'll be moving around by Land Rover through thick jungle, some of which may be mined. I want you all to remember that, whereas all security precautions have been taken by the Government to ensure our safety, they cannot guarantee it one hundred per cent for the simple reason that there is a bloody civil war on. I also want you to remember that you are doing this in the service of the United Nations and that alone should constitute your reward. Any questions?'

★   ★   ★

'So I suppose I'll have to release you again,' muttered Ronald Heller.

Galina looked at her Chief Interpreter squarely and said, with a slightly superior smile, 'Yes, I guess you'll have to.'

There were a few moments of silence, during which he appeared to busy himself with the papers on his desk. While he shuffled his files around, she sat observing him with a mixture of contempt and pity. His fat neck protruded from his tight collar and there were stains of grease on his tie and suit, and she noticed that there was dirt under his fingernails. She felt a shiver of revulsion when she remembered how once, during a mission to Kenya, he had made a clumsy pass at her. When she turned him down in favour of a younger, better-looking and less insecure colleague, he had written her a crazy love letter, begging to be allowed to take her out. Sometimes she regretted having torn it up, especially when she had one of her many arguments with him over his incompetence in running the section. But then, blackmail was not her forte, and she wanted to keep her hands clean.

'When are you leaving?' asked Heller. His breathing, she noticed, was laboured.

He was probably some fifty pounds overweight.

'I told you, October 16th, but I would like a few days' vacation before, so I can get ready.'

He sighed. 'Well, there is a lot of work and . . . '

She smiled sweetly. 'Well, the Secretary General wants me in good shape and you would say that is a priority, wouldn't you?'

'I suppose so,' he answered, resigned.

'Thank you. I can always count on your understanding, Mr Heller.' She could not help the sarcasm. The man was so damn servile. He and Brian Crowley ought to get together, she reflected, as she left her boss's office, true dyed-in-the-wool United Nations bureaucrats, incompetent and obsequious.

She passed Donna and Maud with the briefest of greetings and hurried out of the building. She had so much to do before her departure for Nicaragua.

★ ★ ★

As she walked out of the main gate, she could discern a familiar tall figure standing at the First Avenue bus stop, holding an enormous bouquet of flowers. She drew level with the man, and looked at him with a mixture of surprise and amusement. Awkwardly, he thrust the flowers at her and then proceeded to crush them as he took her in his arms, as if afraid she would get away. 'I love you, Galina, I need you. I've been miserable without you,' he whispered into her hair. 'I've come to say I'm sorry for having been so selfish and so unsympathetic,' whereupon he kissed her long and passionately, under the bemused eyes of some of her colleagues who were leaving the building at the same time as Galina.

'It's all right,' she said, when she managed to catch her breath, 'I've been selfish, too, Bill. It's just that the demands of my work, all my travelling, and the sheer stress of having to stay on top of things in this city often make me forget how much we need each other.' She smiled and stretched her arms as far as they could go to reach his neck.

'In future, I'll try and be more understanding, darling,' he said softly, stooping to let her hug him. 'I've been doing a lot of thinking these days, since our wretched argument at Citicorp, and I've realized just how important your work is to you. I promise you, sweetheart, that when we're married you'll go on working, even when the kids arrive. I won't expect you to bury yourself in a pile of diapers and reams of bridge and gossip in Westchester. You'll have a full-time nanny and a maid and whatever other help you need. Just say you'll still marry me. Oh, and I take back what I said about Commies at the UN. That was benighted of me, I didn't really mean it and I'm sorry I gave you the impression I was such a hick.'

Galina stood there, listening to his torrent of apologies and thinking that Bill was a good man, and that most of her single girlfriends would have given their right arm to be so loved. Somehow, she felt she ought to love him more, but she

225

knew she couldn't. And yet, she was sure they would have a solid, caring marriage, a marriage that worked. Yes, she decided, Nicaragua would be her last mission, after which she would settle down and take care of the man who loved her so faithfully.

New York, early October, 1986

Manuel Mendez sat on the deck of the Staten Island ferry and watched the illuminated Statue of Liberty come into view. Come to me, ye poor, ye tired, ye huddled masses. Well, he had come to her, to the beacon of hope in the land of opportunity when Fidel had first released him from jail and dumped him on the United States with his fellow *marielitos*. At first, and for a brief spell, he had really tried to go straight, to get a job and to study law, to defend people like himself who had grown up in the streets of Havana and taken to crime because in Castro's socialist paradise there was no other choice. If you starved, you stole, and if you stole you were a parasite, and, as everybody knew, parasites lived off other people and therefore deserved to end up in jail or cutting sugar cane or both.

Neither the Communist nor the capitalist society had given Manuel Mendez a break. Well, if he was going to be a misfit, then he might as well, he figured, take a leaf out of the capitalist book on private enterprise. So he had gone into drugs, and drugs had led him to gun-running. The rest had been recent history, of which his providential meeting with that idiot Brian Crowley had been a highlight. For months, through Brian, he had kept the United Nations diplomatic community well supplied with heroin and cocaine and the latest and most powerful, crack. His little trade had led to a brisk business in weapons, on which he had developed a real public relations network. And then there had been that Bob Bailey, a real godsend.

Manuel smiled, fingering the gift-wrapped box of cigars he was carrying. To think such a small, innocent-looking

227

package would stand him in such good stead.

'Hello, Manuel. Nice evening for October, isn't it?' Basil Crimer had appeared out of nowhere. He sat down next to the Cuban and took out a packet of Dunhills. 'Cigarette?'

Manuel took one and Crimer lit it for him. 'Nice,' said Manuel, 'but I prefer cigars.'

'Really? What a coincidence. So do I.'

'Our friend Brian go to Nicaragua?'

'So he tells me. Very soon, I believe.'

'You think he like to take a box of cigars for someone there?'

'Yeah, why not. He's a nice guy, always ready to do you a favour.'

'Here it is, then.'

'Thanks. How much?'

'That okay, man. See you soon.'

The ferry docked with the loud clang of ancient machinery and Manuel Mendez disappeared down the ramp leading to the Manhattan terminal. That was the last Basil Crimer ever saw of the *marielito*.

Managua, mid-October, 1986

On Wednesday, October 15th, Air Guatemala flight number 53 landed at Managua International Airport. Among the passengers was one Pedro Ramirez, Cuban businessman who had come to Nicaragua to negotiate a deal with the Government for medical equipment Cuba had recently acquired from the Soviet Union at cut price and was reselling to sister Socialist Nicaragua at a hefty profit. The fact that the equipment was several years out of date did not seem to preoccupy either seller or buyer. Pedro Ramirez, who was the intermediary, had been chosen for the job because of his total trustworthiness, so a letter of introduction to Managua business circles read. He had, of course, been careful to show the letter, along with his official Cuban Foreign Ministry credentials at the airport. The immigration official had been so impressed that he had never even thought of asking him to open his briefcase. Had he done so, he would have been intrigued by an electronic blood pressure machine that Pedro Ramirez — or Manuel Mendez, his real name — happened to be carrying as part of his sales demonstration equipment.

16

New York, October 16th, 1986

Friday, October 16th, 1986, dawned crisp and clear, a gentle day in the New York autumn, a welcome interlude between the city's humid tropical summer and its storm-swept winter. Before it ended, that tranquil Friday would be marred by unexpected tragedy and in the public mind forever associated with the death of one of the world's most outstanding and respected figures, Leo Anders, fifth Secretary General of the United Nations. It was all the more tragic a death because it occurred while Secretary General Anders was on his way to Nicaragua on a neutral observer mission as guest of the Government of President Daniel Ortega. Along with Anders, the Organization mourned the loss of a dozen senior staff, including Brian Crowley, personal assistant to the United Nations Chief

Executive, killed when the plane carrying them crashed on approach to Managua International Airport.

New York,
October 16th, 1986, 11 a.m.

Brian Crowley had been having a hard time trying to close his suitcase, which, in addition to his clothes, brimmed with all manner of pills, potions and ointments to cover any eventuality from fever to flatulence. 'Damn,' he swore, 'and I meant to travel light.'

Basil Crimer, wearing a silk dressing gown and sipping his morning coffee, peered at his lover over the half-moon glasses he wore for reading. 'Oh Brian,' he said evenly, 'I meant to ask you this before but it just slipped my mind, I am afraid.'

'Yes, what is it, Bob?'

'Well, you see, I've got this friend at the local United Nations office in Managua and I was wondering if you would take a little something for him.'

'Well . . . ' demurred Brian.

'Please. Will you do it for me, please, just this once? Actually, you might like to meet my friend, who is very good looking and sexy and, now that I think of it, will probably be very nice to you.'

Brian's resolve, never very great, began to melt. 'Well, all right. What is it?'

Crimer yawned and got up as if he had all the time in the world. He went into the bedroom and emerged a few minutes later with the box of cigars Manuel had given him on the Staten Island ferry.

'Here you are,' he said handing the box to Brian, 'my friend's name is on it, so you'll have no difficulty finding him.'

Brian took the gift, consisting of a dozen choice Cuban cigars, one of which contained a charge capable of destroying the plane carrying him and Secretary General Anders to Nicaragua a little later that same day.

Managua, October 16th, 5 p.m.

It was nearly four forty five. Any minute now, Manuel expected to hear the exchange between the control tower and the pilot of the Secretary General's plane. He was sitting on the floor of the stifling hotel room at Managua airport hunched over his radio receiver and trying hard to ignore the heat, the filth and the flies. He was gasping for air, but did not dare open the shutters. At all costs, he had to protect himself from the prying eyes of the police and military patrolling the airport.

★   ★   ★

The receiver was tuned into the control-tower frequency and Manuel was fiddling with the dial, although he could hear nothing but hissing through the earphones he kept tightly clamped on his head. Next to him was the electronic blood-pressure machine, ostensibly part of his demonstration sales equipment, and in actual fact a

234

device housing a transmitter designed to activate the bomb the unsuspecting Brian Crowley was carrying in his luggage.

Four-fifty. Where was that damn plane? He was keen to get the hell out of there, collect the money that Crimer had deposited for him in a Zurich bank, and start living. He indulged in a bit of daydreaming, wondering where he would retire. Tahiti, perhaps, or Bora Bora. As far away as possible, where no one knew him.

There it was, the crackling over the earphones he had been expecting. 'Managua control tower, Managua control tower, United Nations Flight One requesting permission to land. Over.'

'United Nations Flight One,' came the answer in heavily accented English. 'Permission granted. Safe landing.'

Manuel pressed the switch on the radio transmitter.

Washington, October 16th, 6 p.m.

One hour later, at six p.m., in a town house in the wealthy neighbourhood of Georgetown, Washington, Basil Crimer picked up the phone. He had been expecting the call since five-thirty and had grown increasingly jittery, wondering whether something had gone wrong, whether Manuel had been caught or customs officials had become suspicious and decided to search Brian Crowley's luggage, even though, as a member of the Secretary General's mission, Brian enjoyed full diplomatic immunity. No, that was not possible, not with the kind of airtight planning von Steuben had put into the enterprise. But Crimer knew full well that the best laid plans can go awry.

The phone rang, wrenching him out of his thoughts, and he pounced on it. When he lifted the receiver, he heard crackling on the line, and the sound was so faint it seemed to be coming from underwater, but the voice was familiar.

'*Patria o muerte. Venceremos,*' Manuel said.

'Well done, Phoenix. No survivors?'

'None.'

'You can collect, then.'

'*Gracias, amigo,*' replied Manuel warmly. Then there was a click and the phone went dead.

New York, October 16th, 5 p.m.

The waves crashed on the shore spewing clouds of spray that the wind carried like so many raindrops, washing over Galina as she took her daily walk on the beach at Montauk Point, the furthest edge of Long Island. For a week now that had been her routine every morning, and she had grown to love the solitude and the silence, broken only by the cries of seagulls fluttering in the October sky. A friend of hers had lent her the house for as long as she needed to recover from the sequels of the peritonitis that had left her totally drained of all strength. She still felt terribly depressed when she remembered how she had welcomed the prestigious assignment to Nicaragua and had prepared for it conscientiously, reading up on the years of the Somoza tyranny, on the rise to power of the Sandinista regime of Daniel Ortega and the civil war that ensued. She had begun to find Central American politics both baffling and fascinating, and had looked forward to witnessing the situation first hand. Instead, that stupid illness had come and fouled everything up, forcing her to give up the assignment. She wondered who Anders had chosen to replace her — whoever it was, he or she would undoubtedly reap the glamour that had so very nearly touched Galina . . .

★　★　★

She still remembered that unbearable pain. A giant hand had been clawing at her insides mercilessly, forcing her into a foetal position with her arms crossed over her belly in a vain effort to lessen the agony. This is ridiculous, she had thought, of all the times to get food poisoning, when I have so much to take care of, what with the Nicaragua mission only two weeks away. It had all been her own stupid fault — she should never have chosen that new seafood place in Greenwich Village which was the talk of the town. Friends from her student days on the West Coast had been in town and she had suggested that restaurant because it had received glowing reviews in some trendy Manhattan magazines, and it had been far from easy to get a reservation. Eventually, after a great deal of begging and cajoling they had managed to find a table and everybody had agreed it had been well worth it — the food had indeed proved superb.

When she had finally succeeded in excusing herself and getting back to her apartment, it had been gone midnight, and she had had a full day's work ahead of her. So she had gone straight to bed, picked up a Soviet novel she had bought on Nikolai's recommendation, *Children of the Arbat*, a harrowing and candid account of repression in Stalinist times. She had read until the print began to dance before her fast-closing eyes and, just as she was slowly letting herself drift into a gentle, restful sleep, it happened. The first stab of pain had left her breathless. I've probably sprained a muscle in dance-class, I must not panic, it will go away if I lie still. But it had not, and it was followed by another and then another blow, just as if she were mercilessly being punched in the stomach. So it went on throughout the night, until she lay on the pillows gasping for air and drenched in sweat.

A fist squeezed her belly hard, then released, only to tighten its hold a few seconds later. This is not going to get better, she had decided, I must call Dr Blum. He had been the family physician for years, and that was why she had his private number and was allowed to phone at all hours, knowing he would always be available.

'Hello,' the doctor's wife had said sleepily.

'Mrs Blum, this is Galina Romanova. Is your husband there? I think I've got a bad case of food poisoning and . . . '

She was going to explain about her

mission, tell Mrs Blum how important it was for the doctor to see her right away, when a violent wave of pain had racked her body. Mercifully, it had been the last thing she remembered for some time.

★   ★   ★

'I don't believe it. You've got to be kidding, Dr Blum.'

'No, unfortunately I am not, Galina.' The doctor sat on the edge of her bed and looked at her sadly. 'It was peritonitis all right. In fact, it still is. The infection hasn't cleared yet.'

'But this is ridiculous. I've got an important official mission for the United Nations coming up in less than ten days.'

'Then you'll tell your boss at the UN that he'd better find a replacement, and fast.'

'But I can't do that. I'm supposed to be going with the Secretary General to Nicaragua and . . . '

'Look, Galina. I've known your family for years, I was very fond of your parents and I just can't let you commit an act of

241

folly, which is what you are about to do. If you had said Europe, I would still have been reticent. But Nicaragua . . . ' He shook his head. 'My dear, dear child. The answer is no, and it will continue to be no even if I have to keep you here by force until that plane has taken off.'

Galina put her head in her hands and sobbed. She had really been looking forward to the trip with Leo Anders. Like her mission to Geneva last year, it was to be a glamorous highlight, a break from routine even if it was fraught with all kinds of hardship. And now she was grounded, forced to sit at home and watch someone else replacing her, and maybe not just on this trip either. Anders would never forgive her. And as for Bill, he would be delighted, of course. Just what he always wanted. She could stay home and have babies.

Dr Blum patted her hand, wondering whether to tell her now or wait until she was fully recovered. The first post-operative laboratory tests on Galina Romanova had come back, showing that internal damage from her ruptured appendix and the ensuing infection was more extensive than he had feared at first. The massive doses of antibiotics pumped into her had only just managed to save her life but tissue scarring would probably leave her permanently sterile.

No, Dr Blum decided, he would not say anything for the moment. There would be time enough later, when she was fully recovered. He leaned over, kissed her tear-stained cheek gently. 'If all goes well and you are a reasonable girl, then you can go home at the weekend. But I'm warning you, Galina, don't even try to go to work for another two weeks at least. If you do, you can find yourself another doctor, because I don't want to be responsible for your death.'

⋆   ⋆   ⋆

She glanced at her watch. Five o'clock. It was time to head back if she was going to make it back to Manhattan for the performance of the Kirov ballet. When she first heard they were coming to town, she had booked and invited Bill along. As far as she was concerned, he had well deserved it — since their reconciliation and all the way through her illness, he had been endlessly solicitous, showering her with all manner of attentions and gifts. As far as he was concerned, Heaven knew he would rather have been watching the Stock Market tickertape than 'Swan Lake', but he had accepted because it was a good excuse to spend an evening with Galina, an evening he hoped to make memorable by asking her to set the date for their wedding.

Washington, October 16th, 6 p.m.

Basil Crimer carefully replaced the receiver. For a brief moment, his jubilant mood made him forget all common sense. He stood up, whistling softly to himself. The tune was 'God Bless America', and he felt like breaking out into full-throated song, but his sense of self-preservation won out and he quietly made for the front door. As he stepped out into the chill

November evening, he could not help thinking about his friend, Senator Wayne Ealing, whose house he had borrowed for a few hours. The Senator had asked for no explanations, convinced as he was that Crimer would be meeting a mistress. Basil smiled. There was another, more interesting twist. Back in the sixties, Senator Ealing had been an ardent supporter of the CIA clean-up operation in Vietnam, during which entire villages had been razed to the ground, killing scores of defenceless women and children suspected by the American Command of harbouring Vietcong guerrillas. The operation was called Phoenix, which had inspired the code name for Manuel Mendez on his Managua mission.

A few minutes after leaving Senator Ealing's house, Basil Crimer was comfortably seated in a taxi on his way to Dulles Airport, where he would catch the first shuttle to New York City and his meeting with Kurt von Steuben.

New York, October 16th, 7 p.m.

Galina sighed, reluctantly turned the strong shower jet off, hastily wrapped an oversized towel around her dripping body, and padded into the living-room to answer the phone. At first, she had not heard it through the steady gush of the water, then she tried hard to ignore it, so pleasant was it to stand there, thinking of nothing, washing the day away. Finally, she realized she would have to answer the shrill insistent little machine that would not leave her in peace.

'Ah, there you are at last, darling.' Bill sounded worried.

'I was in the shower. I have just got in from the Island, First Avenue traffic was beastly, and if we are to make it to Lincoln Center . . . '

He cut her off impatiently. For all his love for her, he had to admit that, like all women, she did tend to blither. 'That's what I was calling you about. Well, partly, anyhow.'

'You can't make it to the Kirov's *Swan Lake*?' she had been looking forward to it, had taken the trouble to book months in advance. When the Kirov ballet was in town, New Yorkers were ready to gun each other down for a ticket.

'I can. Just. But we'll have to have dinner after the show and not before, as we had planned. Can you meet me in the lobby of the New York State Theater at, say, a quarter of eight?'

'Fine. See you there.'

Drying herself with quick, vigorous movements, she walked into the kitchen, opened her enormous fridge, empty except for a bottle of Stolichnaya, a small glass and a large pot of Beluga caviar. She poured the vodka into the glass, added an ice cube, took the caviar, some crackers and went back to the living room. She glanced at her watch and decided she had time to watch the seven o'clock news.

She switched on the television and, as she listened, she forgot the vodka, the caviar and the ballet altogether.

'Although sabotage can't be ruled out, the authorities will have to wait until the black box is found to confirm their suspicions,' Dan Rather was saying, as a picture of charred plane debris flashed on to the screen. 'All we can do for the moment is mourn the loss of United Nations Secretary General Leo Anders and the team accompanying him on his mission to Nicaragua . . . '

So Leo Anders was dead and she could have been dead with him. She closed her eyes, not wanting to think any more. But images kept coming back to her mind, like so many stills replayed over and over again . . . Leo Anders, the man of peace, Leo Anders who had got too big for his boots and refused to be a yes-man, and for that he had been destroyed. Yes, she thought bitterly, Leo Anders has paid for his courage, paid with his life in war-torn Nicaragua, just as his predecessor Hammarskjöld in Northern Rhodesia all those years ago . . .

My imagination is running wild and loose. I must not get carried away.

What she did not know was that she was within a hair's breadth of the truth.

She stared at the screen. *Boje moi.* Was it possible? No, how could he be here, in

248

New York, when he was supposed to have been back in Moscow . . .

'Ambassador Golovin, will you, as the new Permanent Representative of the Soviet Union to the United Nations, please tell us whether you knew Secretary General Anders?'

'Indeed,' said Nikolai Golovin in his impeccable mid-Atlantic English. 'When I first came to the United Nations as an interpreter some years ago, Leo Anders impressed me as a fair man who always stood up for his beliefs, a rare specimen in this world . . . ' Galina smiled. Just like Nikolai, diplomatic and noble. Nikolai the cosmopolitan, the perfect spokesman for Gorbachev's *glasnost*. So he was now Ambassador. Of course, she had been away on sick leave, she had no way of knowing he was here.

Well, she would see him soon enough at the UN. I wonder what I'll say to him. Mr Ambassador, what a pleasure to meet you again . . . She picked up her glass with such a shaky hand that she spilled most of the vodka. Damn! Her nervousness, she realized, was now only vaguely connected with the Secretary General's death.

A tidal wave of confused emotions swept over Galina. She just stood rooted to the spot, fighting to steady her nerves. She wondered how long it would be before she ran into Nikolai in the Delegates' lounge on the second floor, the usual meeting place at the UN. Probably not very long, she thought sadly, he will see to it, just as he did a year ago . . .

★ ★ ★

The shuttle from Washington landed at New York's La Guardia Airport on time on the evening of October 16th. Basil Crimer had no luggage, which made things all the easier. Outside the terminal, he caught a taxi and told the driver to go to the Pierre Hotel, where von Steuben had booked a room for him. Nothing but the best, he thought, trying to keep his euphoria from bubbling over. He felt such a high, knowing it was done, Anders was dead and gone and there was nothing, absolutely nothing that stood in his way

250

now. He was really looking forward to seeing Kurt and Anneliese, scheduled to arrive some time tomorrow. First, however, he needed a good dinner — Lutèce, the top French restaurant in New York would do — and a good night's sleep. There was so much to be done.

Geneva, October 17th, 2 a.m.

Long after Anneliese had gone to sleep, Kurt von Steuben sat in his library at Cologny, pondering the day's events. It all seemed like a dream he would wake up from, a beautiful dream of power and freedom, all made possible by Leo Anders' death. Tomorrow, he and Anneliese would be leaving Geneva for New York to attend that idiot's funeral. And then, and then . . .

Damn, he had almost forgotten. In his enthusiasm over the report of the plane crash on the evening news, he had totally omitted a crucial bit of business.

He picked up the phone and dialled a

Zurich number. Manuel's secret would die with him.

Zurich, October 17th, 7 p.m.

Manuel Mendez cruised down Zurich's elegant Limmatquai in his rented Toyota Corolla. The many long delays and the four connections he had had to make on his Managua — Zurich flight had landed him at Kloten Airport too late that day to collect the two hundred and fifty thousand dollars Crimer had had deposited in the bank for him, but Manuel did not mind. He would find a fancy hotel, where he could stay overnight, and the next day he would pick up his payment and be on his way to the South Pacific. At long last, he was beginning to live.

Just ahead of him, he saw a red and white awning, under which stood a liveried doorman. As he eased his Toyota to a gentle stop in front of the building, he could make out the name *Zurich Plaza* in gold lettering over the revolving door. Inside, he could discern the crystal

252

chandelier that glittered like diamonds in the lobby. A symbol of my new life, gloated Manuel, getting out of the car. He would spend the night in this ritzy establishment, and enjoy the luxury it offered, which he felt he well deserved.

At the reception desk, he produced a passport in the name of Luis Campos, Cuban businessman residing in Miami. Once more, he marvelled at the perfect forgery his friend Nino had crafted. This document, like Nino's other masterpiece that he had used to get into Nicaragua, was so finely worked that even the usually suspicious Swiss immigration officials at the airport had waved him through after a perfunctory check.

The receptionist examined the passport, returned it to Manuel, and smiled broadly. 'Room 515, sir. Any luggage?'

'Jus' my flight bag. I'll only be stayin' overnigh'.' Manuel was pleased at the new, commanding tone of his voice. He sounded important, prosperous.

'Very well, sir. The bell-hop will see you to your room.'

A young uniformed boy sprang out of

nowhere and materialized by Manuel's side. 'This way, sir. Please follow me.'

As he started down the thickly carpeted lobby, Manuel marvelled at his good fortune. It was great to be treated like the gentleman he was meant to be . . .

'Mr Campos, just a moment, Mr Campos. Mr Campos.'

It took Manuel a few seconds to realize it was him the receptionist was calling. He swung around, alarmed. 'Yeah?'

'Mr Campos, is that your red Toyota parked in front of the hotel?'

'Yeah. Why?'

'Because that's a no parking zone, sir. If you wish we can park your car for you in our underground garage.'

Manuel hoped the relief did not show on his face. For a few wretched moments, he had felt his heart thundering against his ribs with the sheer terror of imminent arrest for murder. He swallowed hard and managed a smile. 'That's fine, man. Yeah, here are the keys.'

'Right, sir. I'll send for the attendant.'

* * *

Had Manuel noticed the white Opel that had discreetly followed him from the airport and had drawn up to the kerb just behind his Toyota, he might have lived to enjoy his rich retirement in the South Seas. But, partly out of fatigue and largely out of a newly acquired feeling of safety, his usual caution, which had saved his life so often before, had totally deserted him.

This is going to be easier than I anticipated, thought the driver and only occupant of the Opel, a sandy-haired young man in his thirties, of totally unremarkable appearance, except for his eyes, light blue and totally devoid of expression. Anyone looking into those eyes involuntarily shivered, for there was no feeling in their cold, appraising stare. They were the eyes of an accomplished murderer and they easily picked out the number on the licence plates of Manuel's car.

Zurich, October 18th, 10 a.m.

Manuel Mendez had had a good night's sleep and he felt refreshed, ready to face what would be a wonderful day. Soon, very soon, he would be a rich and free man. After a hearty breakfast, he paid the hotel bill and took the lift to the underground garage where he promptly located his Toyota Corolla.

He got in, stretched lazily in the driver's seat, then put the key in the ignition and turned.

The blast stunned him and, before he even had time to scream, he felt flames engulf him. Like Brian Crowley's, his last moments were made of intense pain as fire charred his helpless body.

17

Vermont, late October, 1986

The Swiss-style chalet was set in acres of woodland, and well hidden from prying eyes by tall pine and birch that reminded the visitor of the landscape of his native Russia. As he drove up to the entrance, the man reflected that it was no time to be sentimental, for he had urgent and important business on hand, business that had to be dispatched quickly and quietly. Those had been the clear instructions he had received earlier that day from Moscow.

He parked his modest two-door Honda and walked up the wooden steps to the front door, carefully glancing around to check that he had not been followed. But he was well and truly alone, not counting the well-concealed television cameras and electronic detector devices that dotted the property. He lifted his hand to knock, and at that precise moment, the door opened as if by magic to reveal a tall, intellectual-looking man whose worn tweeds gave him a professorial air.

'Welcome, Mr Rybakov,' said the host, whose name was Boyd Whelan and who held the impressive title of US Assistant Secretary of State for International Organizations. 'I trust you have not had too much trouble finding this place. Do come in, please.'

'Thank you, Mr Whelan,' answered Soviet Deputy Foreign Minister Vadim Rybakov. 'Beautiful property you have here. I wouldn't mind a *dacha* like this back home.'

'Nice, isn't it?' smiled Whelan. 'Something to look forward to during my hectic week in Washington. Well, I'm sure you know all about the rigours of Government service. Take a seat.' Boyd Whelan led his guest into a large den, elegantly furnished with soft pearl-grey leather armchairs and a coffee-table carved out of California redwood. At that moment, Rybakov would have given his nearest and dearest to live like his capitalist counterpart.

'Do sit down, Mr Rybakov.' Vadim nodded, gratefully sinking his stocky frame into the upholstery which seemed made to receive him. 'We don't have much time, so let's get down to business right away. Oh, forgive me, I'm such a bad host. Would you like a drink?'

Rybakov smiled, revealing a fine set of gold-capped teeth. 'Thank you, yes. Scotch, please, on the rocks.'

'Fine.' Whelan poured his guest and himself a generous measure from a crystal decanter on the table. He raised his glass. 'Cheers.'

'Good health,' responded Rybakov, draining his glass in one long gulp.

'Well, Mr Rybakov? What does your Government say about our proposal?'

'We agree,' replied Vadim succinctly, for he had always believed in coming straight to the point. 'We shall not contest Kurt von Steuben's election despite his Nazi past.'

'You mean because of it,' corrected Whelan affably. 'We shall so instruct our respective Ambassadors at the United Nations.'

'I understand we will let him complete his term of office.'

'You understand right, Mr Rybakov. He will be allowed to remain Secretary General until 1991, under our discreet supervision and control. Of course, there are one or two minor points to clear up before we proceed.'

Rybakov's thick dark eyebrows went up, making him even more of a Brezhnev look-alike than he actually was.

'Well,' continued Whelan, in response to the unspoken question. 'Spheres of influence, for instance. Von Steuben will be virtually under our thumb and we'll be able to carve up the Secretariat pretty much any way we choose . . . '

Rybakov waved his hand dismissively. 'No problem. We can decide that later. More importantly, we want to make sure von Steuben pays for the atrocities he committed in Kiev in 1942 . . . ' Rybakov's face hardened with pure hatred. His wife's entire family had been wiped out when the Nazis razed whole areas of the Ukraine to the ground.

'Don't worry, Mr Rybakov, we've taken care of that. There's someone besides our two Governments with more than a passing interest in Kurt von Steuben . . . '

New York, late October, 1986

Kurt von Steuben delivered a moving eulogy for Secretary General Leo Anders. 'In Leo Anders,' concluded the Director of the United Nations Office at Geneva, 'we mourn a man supremely devoted to the noble ideals of the United Nations, to the defence of human rights wherever they are flouted, to the maintenance of international peace and security. We have indeed lost a man of integrity, a distinguished leader who was able to rise above national interests to protect the loftier aspirations of mankind. Above all, Secretary General Anders was a man of vision, a good man. Your excellencies, distinguished delegates, ladies and gentlemen, I ask you all to rise and observe a minute of silence in honour of his memory.'

In the General Assembly Hall hung with black crepe, the diplomatic corps stood up and remembered a man who, despite having pleased only a few and offended many with his outspoken courage, would be recalled as someone who had forever left a mark on the world organization. Some were relieved he was dead at last because he could make no further trouble by denouncing the abuses of their governments, others were sorry because they justly felt the United Nations was all the poorer for the loss.

In the booths above the huge hall, Galina and her colleagues stood and remembered a boss who had been kind and gentle and fair, who had been unwilling to become hostage to the cumbersome, inhuman bureaucracy that so often turned the Organization into an inefficient, lumbering giant. Galina's restless eyes ran over the delegates assembled below her, studying them as if in a theatre. For that was what the United Nations had become, she reflected, a theatre of the absurd. Down in the row of seats assigned to the Soviet delegation, Galina spotted the newly appointed Ambassador, Nikolai Golovin, and caught her breath at the power of her longing for him which caught her and held her in its grip and would not let her go. She saw him turn, whisper something to one of his aides, and she could distinguish his features clearly — they were as real to her, and as riveting, as they had been all those months ago in Geneva. If anything, rank agreed with him, she thought — he carried his new authority naturally, as if born to it. For a few moments, she was conscious of fighting her overwhelming impulse to go down into the hall and talk to him, tell him that she had not forgotten their brief time together in Geneva . . .

'Something the matter, Galina?' asked her colleague Marcia, a sweet American girl with a cute freckled face and about as much knowledge of the world as Sleeping Beauty.

'No, no, it's all right, I'm just a bit upset, you know, about Anders.'

'Believe me, I feel the same way. I think we all do. He was such a fine man.'

263

'Yes, wasn't he?' said Galina absently. And that is probably why he died, she added to herself.

★　★　★

One week later, on October 24th, United Nations Day, the Security Council elected Kurt von Steuben Sixth Secretary General of the United Nations. From the outset, it became clear that he did not face any serious competition from the two runners-up, a Peruvian diplomat with a record distinguished only by his steady and assiduous connivance with his government's human rights abuses and a Bulgarian jurist mainly remarkable for his prodigious consumption of vodka which well matched his no less prodigious zeal in the prosecution of political dissidents. A few United Nations old-timers remarked that it was interesting that Kurt von Steuben faced no opposition whatsoever from any of the five Permanent Members on the fifteen-nation Council — even the two superpowers, the United States and the Soviet Union, cast their crucial votes for him. In explaining their stand as was customary after the round of voting, delegates — including Soviet Ambassador Nikolai Golovin — widely praised the candidate for his distinguished record as Director General of its Geneva Office, and as a champion of fundamental human rights and freedoms, an accolade also conferred by his official biography, circulated to representatives of one hundred and fifty-six Member States.

The General Assembly promptly rubber-stamped the Security Council election and so Kurt von Steuben, former Nazi SS officer and new United Nations Secretary General, moved into the office once so fittingly occupied by his much worthier predecessor Leo Anders, the man he had murdered.

★   ★   ★

'Guess what, Galina. Do you know who our new boss is?' asked Jean de la Fontaine, waving an official circular in her face. As soon as she had seen Jean walk into the interpreters' lounge, Galina had made a vain attempt to flee the premises, for he was an incurable talker in the best French tradition, that is, endlessly and vaguely philosophical. Proudly, he asserted he loved intellectual discourse, and his idea of a mental orgasm was to indulge in *l'esprit carté-sien*. Even his colleagues in the French booth dreaded seclusion with him for the duration of a meeting. Having collared his victim, he could become positively deadly in his philosophical constructs, firing them in relentless volley. Galina realized that they were alone in the lounge and in a fit of helpless panic, understood she was hopelessly lost.

Strangely, though, Jean seemed in no mood for his usual bout of philosophical debate. He was, Galina noticed with surprise, actually indignant. 'Amazing, *vraiment étonnant*,' Jean held forth. 'Of all the qualified people here at the United Nations, the Secretary General cannot find a single person to appoint as Under Secretary General for Conference Services. So what does he do? He appoints a rank outsider, a certain . . . ' Jean referred

266

to his circular, 'a certain . . . Basil Crimer who, it says here, has had a long and distinguished career as an international civil servant, and most especially, a particularly rich and brilliant background as Senior Interpreter for the State Department ideally suiting him for a post where experience in international diplomacy has to blend with technical and linguistic skill.'

'Give me that paper.' Galina nearly leapt out of her seat.

'Hey, cool it, what's the matter?' Jean stepped back, raising his arms defensively.

'I'm sorry, Jean, I didn't mean to be rude,' she apologized. 'May I see the circular, please?'

'Sure.' He handed it to her.

The print seemed to jump out at her. She read it several times, unable to believe her eyes. Yes, it was true. Yes, Crimer now headed the Department of Conference Services and in that capacity he was her and Heller's boss, answerable only to the Secretary General himself.

She shook her head in sheer disbelief. 'But I don't understand, Jean, I just don't understand any of it. It has always traditionally been a Soviet post. Why would an American, a rabid anti-Communist at that, be allowed to occupy it? Why would the Soviet Government condone such an invasion of their territory?'

For the next few days, indeed weeks, Galina's question was endlessly echoed by the staff at Headquarters. It seemed that the whole of the United Nations, particularly the Department of Conference Services, buzzed with rumour, speculation and hear-say. Why had the new Secretary General passed up highly qualified candidates within the Organization to appoint an outsider, known for his anti-Soviet ideas, of which he had made no secret while working for the State Department? Why had the Soviet delegation appeared to accept the appointment calmly, without so much as a murmur of protest? Under Secretaries General were, after all, political appointees whose designation had to clear many a hurdle, not the least of which happened to be the approval of the Member State whose particular sphere of influence happened to cover the Department involved. Conference Services was, as Galina had rightly pointed out to her colleague Jean de la Fontaine, a Soviet-run section and had been so since the founding of the United Nations back in 1945. At that time, the Soviet Union and the United States, the two most powerful victors to emerge from World War II, had carved up the fledgling Organization into areas of dominance. Thus, Political and Security Council Affairs had gone to the Soviet Union and its allies, whereas General Assembly Affairs to the United States and its Western partners. And so on down the line, in an unspoken exercise in diplomatic etiquette which had never been questioned, much less breached.

Until Basil Crimer's appointment.

★   ★   ★

Eventually, rumour died down and it was once again business as usual at the United Nations, where the staff, Galina sadly observed adapts to just about everything. From colleagues, she learned that Heller had been one of the first visitors to Crimer's office to congratulate the new appointee. True to form, she thought, with not a little bitterness. Idly, she wondered whether Basil Crimer would remember their difficult relationship back in Geneva and what the consequences of his hatred of her would be — somehow, she felt it was just a question of time before she felt the full brunt of his inexplicable resentment and, oddly enough, that certainly did not bother her in the least. She was so royally sick of the United Nations, of all that international life she had once considered so very glamorous and alluring. One short year, which had culminated in Leo Anders' tragic death, had been enough to shatter the last vestige of her idealism. She now saw the Organization for what it was; a hollow, pompous exercise in monstrous hypocrisy, a useless and expensive sham.

★   ★   ★

She lay awake nights, turning all these things over and over in her tired mind. Crimer's appointment did not make any sense, but then neither did von Steuben's. It had all happened so quickly, before anyone had the chance to think. Somehow, they had all jumped on von Steuben's bandwagon and stayed there, praising his record, extolling his selfless courage in standing up for his oppressed compatriots back in 1939, when Hitler's hordes had invaded his beloved native Austrian soil. That was, after all, what his official biography said.

With a sense of growing disquiet, she recalled her fleeting glimpse of Crimer in von Steuben's car at the Palais des Nations in Geneva. Of course, there were all sorts of deals made at the United Nations between the most unlikely people. But still her uneasiness would not be laid to rest. What had those two promised each other? Who did they sacrifice to get to the top? Who were they really, Basil Crimer and Kurt von Steuben?

She had to admit to herself that if there

was a cover-up, it had to be a very well orchestrated plan, leaving no loopholes, or at least not obvious enough loopholes that would lead to exposure. If Von Steuben and Crimer were indeed guilty of foul play, they had presumably been careful enough to cover their tracks, so that they would always come clean. Yet some facts were public knowledge, or at least public rumour. Galina recalled a magazine article she had read months ago, reproducing allegations that had appeared in the European press regarding Director General von Steuben's involvement in Nazi war crimes. It was peculiar that, just as the story had appeared, so it had died, presumably a very unnatural death. Grimly, she wondered if that had been Leo Anders' fate, too.

As she lay awake nights, an idea began to form in her mind, an idea of such implications that at first she rejected it out of hand. But it returned again and again, until she was forced to heed its call. There was only one source that could begin to answer her many questions about the new Secretary

General: the confidential files on United Nations staff. These files, not even accessible to the Organization's employees, contained information gleaned by private and public institutions about a staff member's life and career, including political affiliations and activities. They were top secret and, as far as Galina knew, impossible to access, short of breaking into the room where they were kept. No, she was definitely no sleuth. If she really wanted to take a look at that file, she would have to devise some means, far more banal and practical than cloak-and-dagger feats which did not suit her in the least.

18

Joe Pulaski hated week-ends. In fact, he was ardently beginning to look forward to Monday morning when he would be taking up his new post in the United Nations Security Division. Instead of standing guard at the gate for eight hours a day come rain or shine, he would be sitting in a comfortable office in the first basement, keeping watch over the staff confidential files. With his new job went an upgrading and a slight salary increase. And do we need it, he thought bitterly, with eight children and the wife pregnant again, although the baby was not even two and it was too soon for her to have another one on the way, whatever the Church said. Why, there he was, bawling his head off again, the spoiled little brat, while his two older sons, aged nine and ten, teased their five-year-old sister by

274

pulling her hair and snatching her toys away. His four teenage daughters were helping their mother lay the table for Sunday lunch and, amazingly enough, even that simple act did not fail to cause the usual sniping and bickering. And all that hell had to be endured, day in day out, in a shabby one bedroom apartment on East One Hundred and Sixteenth Street, right in the heart of Spanish Harlem, where the local Puerto Rican thugs never let his own kids forget that they were Polish.

Joe looked at his wife sadly. At thirty-five, she looked sixty, her figure destroyed by too many pregnancies, the prettiness gone from her flabby face. He could still recall how he had met her, voluptuous sixteen-year-old Maria, at a local Church dance, how he could not wait to ram it up her the minute he laid hands on that fullness, straining under the tight dress. Father Stefan told him in no uncertain terms he had to marry her first, and so Joe Pulaski did, and by the time he realized he did not love her, the first two kids had been born. For Joe had always had more brawn than brain, and maybe that was why he had enlisted in the New York City Police. That way he was free to beat up the Blacks and Puerto Ricans who molested his kids. In the end, the work got too rough and dangerous for him, so with a couple of knife wounds to show for his record, he joined United Nations Security, where all he had to do was look important and check passes. If only that stingy Organization paid better, everything would be coming up roses. Well, maybe this new job was a sign of times to come, maybe he could expect a series of promotions from now on. Although not bright, he was a good, solid employee, always eager to please his bosses, always ready to oblige, running little errands for the Chief of Security or doing overtime. And now he could reap the reward for his officiousness . . .

★ ★ ★

Early on a Monday morning, Galina Romanova walked into the United Nations Security Office. Finally, after days of indecision, after constantly turning the choices open to her in her mind, she was clear and lucid about what she wanted to do. Of course, it involved a calculated risk, but she was prepared to take it because it ultimately seemed to her that no sacrifice was great enough to know the truth. There were times when she honestly wondered why she could not be like everybody else, why she invariably had to complicate her life. Bill had once told her that she was always out looking for trouble, and maybe he had been right. Somehow, though, she could not help herself, could not help engaging in this crazy quest for the truth because she felt it was the least she owed Leo Anders.

'Hi, sweetheart.' Tom, the guard on duty, was a six-foot former black cop from Harlem, and one of Galina's favourite people at the United Nations.

'Hi, Tom, great to see you.'

He beamed broadly. 'Great to see you too, Miz Lucy.' Miz Lucy was Tom's nickname for Galina, because her blonde, fragile looks always reminded him of a delicate Southern plantation belle. 'And 'what can I do for you?'

'Well, actually I think I'll let you off easy, Tom. I just realized I've lost my pass and I need another one.'

'Sure thing, honey, won't be a minute. Just take a seat.'

While Tom was busy making out her new identity badge, Galina carefully studied the daily assignments of the security staff, clearly posted on the wall in front of her. She ran down the list of names and the corresponding areas each guard was supposed to man, until she came to one that made her sit up and take notice: Pulaski, Joseph — Confidential Files, Office 135, First Basement. Wonderful. She knew Joe Pulaski, and was as friendly to him as to the other security guards, with whom she always exchanged a bit of light banter, a welcome relief in the solemn atmosphere of the United Nations. Joe had often been assigned to the General Assembly Hall, where Galina regularly worked, and she remembered his flat smiling features and his tiny blue eyes that would always roam over her figure whenever she went out for one of her breaks. He had always struck her as a man of limited intelligence, which of course did not mean that he would readily agree to her request. In fact, he might think she was downright crazy, but Joseph Pulaski's opinion of her did not remotely bother her.

Tel Aviv, November 1986

When Colonel Ari ben Levi had first been summoned back to Mossad Headquarters, interrupting his long week-end by the Dead Sea — the first holiday he had enjoyed in months — his immediate temptation was to turn the new assignment down. It was with some difficulty and a great deal of regret that he had extricated himself from hours of torrid lovemaking with Barbara Mellors, the star American television reporter who had proved as brilliant in bed as she had when interviewing him. Barbara had long blond hair, a stunning figure and enough tricks up her sleeve to make the most hardened Israeli sabra forget his devotion to the

Jewish State. And, in his classy *schiksa*'s arms Colonel ben Levi had almost forgotten, until the urgent summons from the Chief of Operations at Mossad.

As his boss explained the nature of the new assignment, Colonel ben Levi was glad that, once again, he had put his country and his work first. For a great deal was at stake, nothing less than just revenge for the horrors endured by his own people. It was a job that had to be done fast and, above all, neatly. But then, not for nothing was he the top operative in the world's best intelligence service.

He glanced at his watch. He had a little over two hours to pack and get to the airport for his flight to New York.

New York, November 1986

Galina spotted Joe Pulaski in the UN cafeteria, having his dinner before going on the evening shift in Confidential Files. She bought a coffee and carefully sauntered over to his table.

'Hi, Joe,' she said cheerfully, a bright

smile on her face. 'May I sit down?'

He looked up, startled. 'Sure thing,' he mumbled with his mouth full, 'please do.'

For a few minutes she was silent, marshalling her thoughts as she watched him spooning the spaghetti bolognese into his mouth, slurping noisily, while tomato sauce ran down his chin. The man had the manners of a pig, and it took all her will-power not to turn away.

'Joe,' she began, 'I came over because I just found out about your important promotion, and I meant to congratulate you and tell you that I'm really pleased for you.'

His small eyes narrowed to slits as he smiled, revealing a mouth full of half-chewed food. 'Thanks,' he spluttered, breaking off a piece of bread and wiping his plate with it.

'It must be very interesting, working with confidential files. I'm sure it's a pretty sensitive job, too.'

'Mmmm,' he mumbled, stuffing the bread into his mouth.

'Well, you deserve it,' she said, hoping

he did not realize how hollow she sounded.

He belched loudly. 'Well, I gotta be going now.' He stood up and collected his tray. 'Thanks for stopping by, anyhow.'

'Wait.' Her voice was a bit too shrill, she realized. 'Joe, wait. There's something I've been meaning to ask you. Do you have a few minutes?'

He glanced at his watch. 'Not really. But if you make it snappy . . . '

'Look, Joe. I know that what I'm going to ask you is not . . . Well, not strictly right, but maybe you can do me a favour and we can keep it a secret between us, something no one ever need know about. See, I am looking for a bit of background on a staff member . . . '

'Why don't you go to the Office of Public Information?'

'That's just it, Joe. All they have is the official biography, and that's very skimpy. I need more, and that's where you come in.'

'I don't follow, lady.' He was beginning to look impatient, clearly keen to get rid of her.

This is going badly, she thought, but I can't backtrack now. 'Well, you are in charge of confidential files, aren't you?'

'Yeah. So what? They are top secret.'

'I know, Joe, and I also know that what I am going to ask you is pretty outrageous and far-fetched and crazy, but I've got my reasons and, believe you me, they are sound.' She took a deep breath and shot the bolt home. 'Do you think . . . do you think you could photocopy the file on Kurt von Steuben for me?'

He whistled softly. 'On the Secretary General? Lady, do you realize that what you are asking is very heavy?'

'Yes, Joe, I am aware of that, but I've got my own compelling reasons . . . '

He looked at her, an idea slowly taking shape in his mind. 'What's in it for me?' he asked slowly.

Galina was thrown off guard. She had not expected that question, and had not thought of anything she could offer Joe Pulaski. 'I don't honestly know,' she answered truthfully. 'All I can tell you is that, by helping me, you might be helping to see justice done at the United Nations.'

Justice. He did not know how he managed to keep a straight face with this far-out dame. You couldn't eat goddamn justice, could you? One thing he knew for sure, that he stood a lot to gain from exploiting this situation to his own best advantage. Yes, his luck had indeed turned.

Galina could see he was hesitating. 'Well, Joe?' she asked anxiously.

'It ain't easy but . . . okay, we'll see what we can do.' Joe smiled at her warmly.

* * *

'Why, thank you, Mr Pulaski. You have proved that you are indeed a loyal international civil servant, and I shall see to it that you are duly rewarded.' Basil Crimer flashed his most engaging smile at Joe, who beamed with pleasure. He was sure he could expect a substantial cash bonus, not to mention another accelerated promotion in exchange for services rendered. It had been well worth it to spend a few minutes listening to that crazy interpreter going on about justice and helping the United Nations and all that crap. Well, he didn't know about helping the UN, but he had surely helped himself.

'I just thought I should waste no time in reporting Romanova to you, sir,' he replied, nervously twisting his cap in his hands. 'I was so stunned she dared approach me with sumpin' like that. I mean, she wanned me to give her a top secret file, and on our Secretary General too . . . ' A note of righteous indignation crept into Joe's voice. 'In my humble view, Mr Crimer, sir, you gotta do sumpin' about that woman before she . . . '

'You've done your duty by reporting the staff member to me,' interrupted Crimer curtly. 'I will decide on the appropriate disciplinary action to be taken against her.'

'My pleasure, Mr Crimer, sir. If you need me again . . . ' 'Then I won't hesitate to call on you. Good day.'

★ ★ ★

After Joe Pulaski left, Basil Crimer sat at his desk for a long time, a puzzled frown on his face. He could not figure out why Galina Romanova would want the file on Kurt von Steuben, but the fact that she did was in itself dangerous — he and Kurt had not come all this way to have the ground pulled out from under their feet by that upstart communist-loving bitch. She was a thorn in his side, that woman, and had been since he met her at the Geneva summit. Always meddling, always pushing herself forward, taking herself for some sort of star. He thought of those pictures he still had, and which so roundly incriminated her and Ambassador Golovin. *Ambassador* Golovin. He snorted. Why, everybody knew Golovin had got the Ambassadorship because he happened to be Gorbachev's bosom buddy. Well, he had to admit helplessly there was nothing in the world he could do about Nikolai Golovin, who, as Soviet Ambassador, was in such a commanding position that everyone in the United Nations Secretariat, and that included Basil Crimer and Kurt von Steuben, owed him obeisance. But there was something he could, and would, do about Galina Romanova. Crimer allowed himself a smile of deep satisfaction. The stupid bitch had hanged herself and all he had to do was tighten the noose.

Producing a small key from his wallet, he unlocked a drawer of his desk and took out the photographs of Galina Romanova that he had obtained from Gaston Thevet back in Geneva. Examining them again, he could not help a smug smile — they were perfectly clear and perfectly incriminating, sure to destroy her reputation and her private life.

Originally, he had thought of threatening her with them if she continued her snooping, but blackmail would look very bad coming from a high United Nations official, and Kurt was sure to rake him over the coals for it. No, he would act behind her back, and just as effectively, for he had it on good authority from the private detective he had employed to research Romanova's life that except for her husband to be, she was totally alone and hence totally vulnerable. Her boyfriend was, moreover, a conservative Wall Street stockbroker and a pathologically jealous man. Once he had evidence of Galina's affair with a Soviet he would turn his back on her forever, and she would be out in the cold and presumably heading fast towards a nervous breakdown.

Still smiling, he took a large envelope, carefully placed the photographs and a brief note inside it, and addressed it to Mr William Hewitt, Rockwell Trust and Guaranty, 25 Wall Street.

As far as he was concerned, Galina Romanova was good and finished.

★　★　★

The immigration official at Kennedy Airport flashed David Cohen the smile she reserved exclusively for VIPs and handed him his diplomatic passport, which accredited him as special envoy to the United Nations General Assembly. 'Have a nice stay in New York, sir,' she said cheerfully.

'Thank you.' David Cohen carefully

put his passport away and left the terminal. Outside, while crowds of irate passengers fought for the few cabs available, he quietly walked to a black limousine discreetly parked in the lot across from the terminal building. As he approached it, he recognized a familiar figure through the tinted bullet-proof glass and opened the door. The man in the driver's seat smiled warmly. '*Shalom*, Ari. Did you have a good trip?'

'*Shalom*, Leon. Yes, the trip was fine, thanks.' Colonel Ari ben Levi, who had just entered the United States under the name of David Cohen, settled in the seat next to his friend Leon Herzog and looked at him fondly. Leon was like a son to him, the son he had never had. They even looked alike — same sharp, hard-edged features, same thick mane of dark hair, except Ari's was streaked with grey.

Leon started the car. 'I'm glad I made it on time to meet you off the plane. There was so much to do at the Mission.'

'Yes, I'm sure they keep you very busy.' Leon was known to be one of the brightest stars on the Israeli delegation to the UN.

'When do we get down to business?' asked Colonel ben Levi. 'I really want to get the job done.'

'In a few hours.' Leon smiled broadly. 'The bastard will pay,' he added, a note of hatred creeping into his voice.

19

New York, November 1986

In the General Assembly's Special Political Committee, Colonel ben Levi, alias
David Cohen, sat with the other members
of his delegation and listened to his
Ambassador's impassioned defence of
Israeli incursions into Lebanon to ferret
out Palestinian terrorists. For three solid
hours, the Arab delegations had pounced
on Ambassador Aaron Epstein with a
concerted barrage of verbal abuse against
his person, his country and Jews in
general. For three solid hours, Colonel
ben Levi had watched Ambassador
Epstein hold his own with dignity, grace
and humour, so that the house could not
help but admire the sheer brilliance of
the Oxford-educated diplomat who was
widely known to be one of his country's
greatest assets on the international scene.
The meeting was running late into the

evening, and so involved were the debaters that the proceedings threatened to drag on for some time yet. Colonel ben Levi checked his watch. Eleven o'clock. It was time. Unnoticed by the rest of the delegates, he quietly slipped out of the conference room and made his way down the darkened corridor to the Confidential Files room.

If all went well, he reckoned he would be able to complete his job well inside half an hour, after which the secret file on United Nations Secretary General Kurt von Steuben would be in safe hands. Never since he had participated in the kidnapping of Nazi criminal Adolf Eichmann in Argentina had Colonel ben Levi felt so exultant.

★   ★   ★

'This meeting of the Special Political Committee is now adjourned.' The chairman brought his gavel down with such quick finality as to preclude further debate.

'About bloody time, too. It's gone

292

midnight. Well, at least tomorrow morning we'll be able to sleep late, if Heller doesn't goof and assign us to a 10 a.m. meeting,' commented Rosemary Scott to Galina. 'I wouldn't put it past him, though.'

Galina looked at her colleague and smiled. Rosemary Scott was a devastatingly pretty English girl with perfect skin, blue eyes and jet-black hair, in addition to a flair for clothes and luxury living. Her arresting good looks, reminiscent of Vivien Leigh's, had fetched her many an admirer, the latest being a rich Arab diplomat who showered her with gifts.

'Would you like a lift home, Galina?' Rosemary's latest whim was a white Porsche and she loved to show it off to her colleagues.

'Thanks, no. You go on ahead. I've got to stop in the office to check my mail,' lied Galina. Even if she had no other business in the building — which she did — she had no desire to become involved with Rosemary and her crowd.

'New York can be a dangerous place,

you know, especially at midnight,' persisted Rosemary.

'Look, Rosemary, I've lived in this city all my life, so I know how to defend myself.' Galina picked up her handbag and made for the door, anxious to get rid of her colleague, who was beginning to get on her nerves.

'Please yourself,' said Rosemary, sounding offended. Who cares, thought Galina, as she left the booth.

The conference room was emptying out as delegates left to report back to their missions on the latest point-scoring in the Israeli-Arab verbal war. Galina took the escalator up to the ground floor and the exit, appearing to be in a rush to leave the building. Then, checking that she was alone, she retraced her steps and walked to the nearest lift. When the doors closed she pressed the button marked 1B and rode down to the First Basement where she emerged in a little-frequented area of the building and quickly covered the few steps that took her to Room 135, Confidential Files.

★　★　★

For three consecutive nights, Basil Crimer had been unable to sleep, despite the ministrations of some of New York's choicest call-girls, who visited him in his newly acquired Park Avenue apartment. So he had taken to staying at the office late, to catch up on paperwork he largely made for himself. If only in that respect, he was the perfect bureaucrat and a true and exemplary international civil servant, a worthy employee of the United Nations.

In his thickly carpeted sanctum, just one floor below the Secretary General's own offices, Basil drank and worried and worried and drank. His worry actually had a name — Galina Romanova. Ever since Joe Pulaski's report on her, Crimer had been trying to do something to stop her. What if the pictures he had sent her boyfriend reached him only *after* Romanova had had a chance to carry out whatever harebrained scheme she had been hatching. It did not take much imagination to conclude, as he had done, that she would bring them all disaster. He had put that argument to von Steuben, without success, for the Secretary General was heavily involved with a succession of visiting Heads of State and Foreign Ministers and had no time for Crimer and his worries. My dear Basil, he had scoffed, you have the imagination of doom. We are sitting pretty, he had added, and now leave me alone, I have an appointment with the Foreign Minister of . . .

The power and the glamour had definitely gone to von Steuben's head, concluded Crimer. Why, the man thought he was invulnerable and was for all the world acting as if he had the past of a saint instead of a Nazi track record. Well, if he would not listen, there was only one option left to protect his friend, himself, and everything they had achieved together.

Somehow, he had to get hold of the file on Kurt von Steuben before anyone else did.

★　★　★

Galina stepped up her pace, as if to dismiss any temptation to turn back at the last minute. She had the option to go home and forget the whole thing, to drop this ridiculous quixotic quest. Maybe Bill was right and she was fighting windmills, and, she added to herself, ruining her job prospects into the bargain. If anyone found out she was so grossly breaching the staff rules as to try and photocopy a top-secret file on the Secretary General, she would face immediate dismissal. But then she was so disenchanted with the way the Organization was being run that losing her job did not unduly bother her. She had no family, no financial responsibilities and she was sure Bill would be only too happy to take care of her.

The door to Joe Pulaski's office was closed, but she could see the light through the frosted glass. As she lifted her hand to knock, she wondered what she would say to him. Maybe it would be best to come straight to the point, to remind him of the talk they had had in the cafeteria a couple of days back.

She tapped on the door lightly and

waited, but there was no answer. Well, he was not expecting her, and it was her own fault for deciding on this surprise visit. It had seemed a good opportunity, as she had happened to be working late and she knew tonight was Joe's late shift . . .

Galina knocked again. Silence. Anxiously, she glanced down the corridor. She tried the handle. The door was unlocked and she pushed it and walked in.

She screamed, but no sound came. She had lost her voice with the shock of what she saw.

Joe Pulaski was sprawled on the ground, his open eyes bulging out of their sockets, his face an ugly mask of pain and death. A rivulet of dried blood stained a corner of his mouth, which was wide open as if, in his last minutes, he had been gasping for breath.

Galina wanted to run, but couldn't. She stood rooted to the spot, frozen in mute horror, knowing she had to get out, out of the building before anyone found her, leave, leave forever, call Bill, break loose from this nightmare . . .

* * *

Basil Crimer left his office and walked to the bank of elevators. It was twelve-fifteen and the building would by now be almost empty, except for a few miserable translators slogging away at the documents just produced by the meeting of the Special Political Committee that had ended a few minutes before. On the way to Confidential Files, he would devise some means to persuade the guard on duty to let him into the archives room.

He was certain Kurt von Steuben would thank him.

20

New York, November 1986

Blind, uncontrollable panic seized Galina. She seemed to be living a sequence straight out of a nightmare, except that the nightmare was real and she had very largely created it for herself. The walls of the tiny office seemed to close in on her, and the smell of death was everywhere. Suddenly, a violent wave of nausea welled up in her and she fought with all her might to suppress it as everything went dark before her eyes and the room began to circle in a kind of crazy dance and she knew she was on the verge of passing out.

With a supreme effort, she struggled to keep conscious and slowly and carefully, supporting herself by placing her hands on the wall, she began to edge towards the door. As soon as she was out of here, out of this building, she would call Bill, she would explain . . .

It was then that she heard the approaching footsteps. She was lost.

If Joe Pulaski had been murdered, and the killer was still around, then he would certainly not hesitate to do away with her too. If she was found out by a security guard out for a random check around the building, she would no doubt be hauled before the Secretary General who would hand her over to the New York Police, and they were sure to hold her as a material witness, if not a prime suspect. She was trapped like a rat in a maze.

* * *

At first, Basil Crimer did his best to ignore the shrill sound of his phone which reverberated insanely in the silence of the corridor where he stood waiting for the elevator. The wild ringing, he knew, came from the phone on his desk, and it sounded desperate and urgent. He didn't know of anyone who could be calling him at this hour, and indeed no one, not even Kurt von Steuben, knew that Basil had taken to spending his nights at the office.

Probably some crackpot, or a delegate's jealous wife dialling the wrong number.

The elevator arrived and just as he was about to step in, Crimer changed his mind. What if someone was calling him with an urgent message — so many weird things seemed to be happening lately, and ever since he had heard the report on Romanova, he had felt he was teetering on the brink of some major catastrophe. Maybe he would do better to answer it — he could always go down to the file-room later. With a heavy sigh, he turned and walked back to his office.

'Mr Crimer?' The girl's voice was disagreeably high-pitched and it irritated him.

'Yes. Who is it?' he barked. 'Do you know it's nearly one o'clock in the morning?'

'My name is Elaine Smith, and I am one of the conference officers with the Special Political Committee. As you probably know, they had a meeting tonight and . . . '

'Yes, I'm aware of it. It ended some time ago. If it's to do with the servicing of the meeting, I'm sure you could have got one of my subordinates to solve the problem for you . . . '

'That's just it, sir. It's a real fluke you are in, because it's important and urgent and neither the Chief of Translation nor the Director of Meetings Service happens to be around at this time of night.'

'I don't blame them,' sighed Crimer. 'Well, go ahead.'

'The Arabic-speaking delegations are furious about what they say are several gross mistranslations in the draft resolution condemning Israel for its annexation policy on the West Bank. In fact, I've got the Syrian Ambassador right next to me, and he insists he's not going to leave the building until he speaks to someone in authority.'

'All right, put him on,' mumbled Crimer, reconciling himself to the inevitable. 'Hello, Your Excellency. What can I do for you? Yes, I do realize that as delegations of Member States you are entitled to the best possible Secretariat service . . . Yes, I do understand it's very difficult to work on a poorly drafted text . . . I'll personally see that it doesn't happen again . . . '

★ ★ ★

Galina felt she was fast losing her grip on reality. Again, she heard those footsteps approaching, then receding, then changing direction, approaching again. Then they moved off and the most perfect silence surrounded her.

She had to move now. It was a risk, but it was her only chance.

She edged towards the door, and peered out into the dimly lit area that surrounded the Confidential Files room. Further on down the corridor, a shaft of light shone on the escalators, which had been switched off for the night. Slowly, she moved out into the darkness of the corridor and crouching almost flush against the wall to keep in the shadow, she made her way towards the emergency stairs.

The door to the stairwell was locked.

The only way out was up the brightly lit escalator.

As she broke into a desperate run, the shriek of the alarm tore the silence around her.

★ ★ ★

'Kurt.' Anneliese shook her husband gently at first, then more forcefully. 'Kurt, wake up. There's an urgent phone call for you.'

'What time is it?'

'Five a.m. Never mind that. It's security at the United Nations and they say it can't wait.'

'Oh what the hell.' Von Steuben reached for the receiver his wife handed to him. 'Hello. Kurt von Steuben speaking.'

'Mr Secretary General, I'm sorry to disturb you in the middle of the night, sir, but there's an emergency. Security guard Pulaski who was on Confidential Files has been found dead.'

Von Steuben sat up, suddenly awake. 'Has the cause been established?'

'No sir, not yet, but we thought we'd better let you know immediately.'

'You did the right thing. I'll be over in a few minutes.'

'What is it, darling?' asked Anneliese sleepily.

'I'll tell you later.'

'Can you at least tell me where you are going?'

'To the office. Go back to sleep.'

Anneliese lay back on the pillows, pouting like a spoiled child. Sometimes she really regretted the move to New York and her husband's new post, which made everything so much more hectic than it had been back in Geneva. True, she and Kurt were now famous and sought after by the richest hostesses in town. Yet the price of all that limelight was that they were rarely, if ever, alone, except at night. And now, she reflected bitterly, the United Nations is taking that away from us, too.

★   ★   ★

Galina reached the lobby of the Secretariat building, forcing herself to slow down to a walk. As far as she could, she

306

wanted to appear to be a a staff member going about her ordinary business, which included late-night work during the hectic session of the General Assembly. The place was deserted, no doubt, she concluded because the guard who was assigned to patrol the area had dashed down to the basement directly he heard the alarm, leaving his duty station unattended.

She felt the slap of the night chill as she stepped out into the plaza and walked across the grounds, virtually deserted at that time of night. Again, she was gripped by a sudden weakness, an overwhelming desire to stop moving, to rest, and again, she fought the impulse with the last scrap of willpower in her.

She would get to the nearest phone and call Bill. No, she would go straight to his apartment in Waterside and let him pull her out of this nightmare she had brought upon herself.

★   ★   ★

'Are you absolutely sure, Dr Merrill?'

'One hundred per cent, Mr Secretary General.' The Director of the United Nations Medical Service, who hated to have his competence questioned, was on the defensive. 'Mr Pulaski died of a heart attack. A massive coronary, in fact.'

'Very strange,' muttered Basil Crimer, lighting his fortieth cigarette of that long night.

'Not at all, sir,' said Dr Merrill, 'considering the way he drank and smoked.' He coughed pointedly, reminding all those present that he had been waging a tireless anti-tobacco campaign for the past five years. 'And by the way, you'd better watch your own smoking, Mr Crimer.'

Crimer glowered at the doctor and put his cigarette out. 'I still don't buy it,' he persisted. 'But even assuming it were true, why the hell did your service, Dr Merrill, give Pulaski clearance for such a sensitive job as Confidential Files?'

'I . . . er . . . I was away at the time.' Dr Merrill's usually red face went purple.

'How convenient,' commented von

Steuben unpleasantly. 'In the course of my tenure I have observed that staff members, especially senior staff members, always happen to be away when the wrong decisions are taken by their subordinates. And this is not the first time it has happened, Dr Merrill, nor is your service the lone offender. As soon as the business at hand is taken care of, I intend to conduct a thorough investigation into Pulaski's appointment, including medical records and clearance.'

'But, Mr Secretary General, sir . . . '

Von Steuben raised a hand to command silence. 'We'll discuss that later, Dr Merrill. Right now, I would like to talk to the man who discovered the body.'

'He's security man Jack Holden,' said Crimer. 'He's waiting outside.'

'Show him in, please.'

In his twenty years at the United Nations, Jack Holden had never enjoyed so much attention from the highest officials in the Organization. A timid, obsequious man in his mid-fifties, he had never amounted to much, until he made that grisly discovery a few hours before.

Now he stood before the Secretary General, sweating profusely and shuffling from foot to foot.

'Mr Holden.' Von Steuben dispensed with pleasantries, superfluous under the circumstances, and in any case, wasted on subordinates. 'I believe you were the first to find Pulaski's body and give the alarm.'

'Yes, sir, Mr Steuben.' In his nervousness, Jack Holden totally forgot the *von* and mispronounced his boss's name as *Stooben*.

'Holden,' snapped the Secretary General with barely contained anger. 'If you can't pronounce my name properly, I suggest you address me by my title, which in any event would be more appropriate.'

'Yes, Mr Secretary General, sir.'

'Continue,' von Steuben snapped his fingers impatiently.

'I was on my night duty in the Assembly Hall area, and then I remembered that I was supposed to check with Joe Pulaski on a point of scheduling.' Holden fervently hoped that he was putting on a convincing act, or at least that the Secretary General was so preoccupied with the night's events that he would not notice the lie. 'So I went down to the basement to see him. I found the door open and Joe ... he was sprawled on the floor, unconscious like, and so before I knew it I threw the alarm switch.'

'You did well, Holden. Did you see anyone loitering in the area?'

'Thank you, sir. No, sir, I didn't.'

'Thank you, Holden. That will be all for the moment. You may leave, but make yourself available to answer any further questions.'

'Right, sir. Just call on me any time.' So his little lie had gone unnoticed after all. Earlier on that evening, Joe Pulaski had promised him some nice porn magazines he kept tightly locked in his desk drawer, and Holden could think of no pleasanter way to while the night away. So he had left his station outside the Assembly Hall and made his way down to the basement, which he briefly reconnoitered just to make sure none of his colleagues were around, particularly one or two he knew who would have been quite happy to report his dereliction of duty to his superiors.

Although neither of them knew it, Jack Holden and Galina Romanova had missed each other by a hair's breadth.

★   ★   ★

Galina paid the cabbie and walked to the front door of Bill's apartment building. In her crazy run she had totally forgotten she was wearing only a light wool dress, and now she realized she was chilled to the bone. As she rode from midtown to Waterside Plaza, it had begun to snow lightly and now thick flakes were rapidly settling on the street. She stepped up her pace, relieved to know she would soon be out of the cold, literally and figuratively, when she reached Bill's apartment. It was so good, so comforting to know that he loved her and would take care of her, that she would never ever have to fight her windmills alone again.

She used her key to let herself into the building, remembering how she and Bill had both enjoyed the life of young trendy

Manhattanites, yuppies who shared bed-space but not living-space, who never put love before career enough to move in together. Well, all this had changed now, she reflected contentedly, they were going to get married and build a family together. This was real, while what had happened back in the UN was not, this was the only normality in the midst of all the madness she had lived in the past few hours.

Mechanically, she got off on Bill's floor and walked to Bill's apartment door and took out her key.

She stood on the threshold, unable to believe her eyes. The flat was brightly lit and Bill was sitting in his favourite armchair by the coffee-table, dishevelled, unshaven and with a half-empty bottle of Scotch next to him.

'Bill . . . ' Something had to be terribly wrong. She had never known him to drink hard liquor at parties, much less at eight o'clock in the morning before work.

'Oh good morning, Galina. I'm so glad you are here. Maybe you can explain what the hell these are.' His voice was slightly slurred.

'I don't know what you mean.'

'Then look. Use your eyes. Oh for Christ's sake, Galina, you've never noticed things at the best of times have you? Well, what do these look like to you?' He held up the photographs that she realized had been next to the bottle of Scotch.

'Pictures,' she mumbled.

'Well done, sweetheart, really quick off the mark. Now come in, close the door which, as usual, you've left open, and kindly explain. Well, come closer. Come on, I want you to take a good look at them, especially as they flatter you. You really do look pretty on them.'

She took the three large photographs he held in his out-stretched hand and saw herself standing in front of Nikolai Golovin's room at the Beau Rivage, looking radiant and anxious.

'Well, Galina? You know, these arrived at my office two days ago, along with an anonymous note which in plain English said you had been having it away with a

Soviet colleague in Geneva. The pictures are of you standing outside his door in the hotel where you both stayed during the summit. Galina, please tell me it's not true.'

She turned away, avoiding his pleading eyes. What was the use?

'Galina . . . '

'I can't tell you it's not true, Bill, because I can't lie to you. In any case, I don't know how to lie.'

'Then it's true?'

She bit her lip. 'Yes, it is.'

Helplessly, he buried his head in his hands, making her want to console him somehow. Only, this time, there was nothing in the world she could do for him. Or for either of them.

'At least tell me then it was just a one-night stand, just an accident, that . . . '

He is so pathetic, she thought, touching almost. She shook her head. 'No, Bill, again, I can't. We spent five nights together, five memorable nights, and don't ask me to renounce what I've done because I won't. I wish I could have told

315

you, I really do, but you would never have accepted it, and I see I was entirely right to keep that affair from you.'

He raised his eyes to her, and in them she saw a look of the purest pain. And the purest hate.

'Get out,' he hissed.

'Bill, I came because . . . '

'I don't care why you came, bitch. All I want to do is be rid of you now.' He laughed nastily. 'Oh, you came all right, you two-bit Russian whore. The trick is, you also came in your Commie friend's arms . . . Oh yeah, did you think I'd never find out, you goddamn cunt, eh? Well, thanks to a well-wisher I have and now I never want to see you again.'

Slowly, she turned and walked away. Why explain anything, why try telling him about Nikolai, or about tonight? It did not make any difference anyhow. She was on her own, as she had been for as long as she could remember.

* * *

She did not remember walking from Waterside Plaza to the upper East Side. All she knew was that she somehow found herself standing in front of her apartment building on Seventy-second and Third without any recollection of how she got there. She stood under the thick, fast snowfall and briefly entertained the idea of going home, then changed her mind. Later. For the moment, she could not face the loneliness of her empty apartment, a bitter reminder that she really had no one left in this world.

Bill had turned her out and she was on her own. Or was she? An idea began to take shape in her mind, a preposterous idea she rejected at first. But then why not? They had been lovers, partners of sorts.

She would try and contact Ambassador Nikolai Golovin.

★ ★ ★

'Sorry, but Ambassador Golovin is out of town.'

'*Kogda ievo zhdete?*' Galina did her level best to keep her voice calm and steady.

'I don't know when to expect him back,' the man said curtly. It was clear he preferred to use English with her, a sign of distrust. 'Who shall I say is calling?' he asked guardedly.

'A friend. It's not important.'

'Would you care to leave message?'

What could she tell Nikolai, she wondered, where to begin?

'I asked if you have message,' the voice snapped impatiently. Probably some tenth-rate underling at the Soviet Mission, terrified of outside callers.

'No. No message,' she answered wearily, putting the phone down.

Aimlessly, she walked down Seventy-second Street, heading towards York Avenue and the East River, a walk she had often taken when her marriage first began to fall apart. After one of those epic, nasty fights with her husband, she would run out of their brownstone on Seventy-fifth and Lexington and head for the river, often trudging through the snow and slush in that one winter ten years ago that had marked the end of her eight-month union with a crazy would-be poet. Again, she had wandered vaguely in the same direction as her mother lay dying of cancer at Lennox Hill hospital, desperate to numb herself against despair. As now.

In the snow-gripped city that was just waking to another hectic day, she was alone. On she walked, for there was no going back, no going back at all. Not to the UN, where sooner or later Crimer would make her his personal victim, as he already had. Somehow, in her bones, she knew it was Crimer who had sent those pictures to Bill. There was no going back to Bill either, no erasing the past, no atoning for her affair with Nikolai Golovin, *Ambassador* Golovin, who, she was certain of it now, would remain forever off limits to her.

An overwhelming indifference to all things swept through her. The liberating aspect of misfortune, of tragedy, was that it set you apart, so that you were no longer bound by the rules that guided ordinary hard-working citizens. And she had set herself apart by her quest for a truth that remained secret and hence her sacrifice was worthless. Bill had been right — she should have stayed home and had babies like everybody else. Well, no doubt he would find someone who was willing to do just that, who would make him a good wife, for she would never really have succeeded. Somehow, from childhood, she had been convinced that hers was not an ordinary destiny and perhaps she had lived to fulfil the feeling that common human happiness was not for her.

When she finally reached the river, she was panting from exhaustion and her face and hands were burning with fever. She leaned over the railing and stared into the cold grey water, as if seeking guidance. Maybe she should contact the news-papers, try and tell someone of her suspicions about Anders' death, maybe someone would listen, there would be an investigation . . . But she had no proof, and she was still lucid enough to understand that without hard evidence, no one would begin to take her seriously.

She had never felt so helpless in her whole life.

Reluctantly, she forced herself to turn back home.

21

Long Island, November 1986

'Another drink, Mr Ambassador?'

'No thank you, Your Excellency. I'm fine.' Ambassador Richard Armstrong had the patrician features and manners of old Boston and the intellectual polish of Exeter and Harvard. Nikolai smiled warmly. He liked this university professor turned diplomat, who was doing a brilliant job as negotiator at the United Nations, and enjoyed their sparring in formal meetings and their friendliness outside them. They had become a star partnership at the United Nations, Soviet Ambassador Nikolai Golovin and United States Ambassador Richard Armstrong, and people watched them, gossiped about them as they would about a legendary movie or ballet partnership. Which, of course, both Nikolai Golovin and Richard Armstrong thoroughly enjoyed.

Nikolai got up and walked to the window. He parted the curtain slightly and looked out at the windswept beach. It was snowing heavily and the sea was steel-grey. He stood there for a few minutes, peering through the fast-falling flakes at the desolate shoreline, then turned back to his American colleague, who was warming his hands at the fire that crackled merrily in the hearth. The tense mood of the two men clashed violently with the cheerful sound and the cosy room decorated with chintz chairs and chintz curtains and pretty pink wallpaper. A room made for middle-class after dinner evenings, thought Nikolai, not for secret diplomatic meetings.

Both men started at the sound of a car driving up. The engine was switched off, a door slammed and almost immediately they heard the chime of the entrance bell. In a flash, Nikolai was by the window. 'That's him all right, Richard,' he said to Ambassador Armstrong, 'thank God at last.'

Richard Armstrong stepped out into the hallway to open the door, and in a few minutes he was ushering his new guest in. 'Do come and warm yourself by the fire and have a drink,' he said pleasantly.

'Thanks, I can sure use it,' smiled Colonel Ari ben Levi, tossing off his woollen cap and brushing the snowflakes off his beard. He was carrying a briefcase which he deposited on the table as delicately as if it were a piece of fragile crystal. 'Good morning, Ambassador Golovin,' he said, inclining his head politely in Nikolai's direction.

'Good morning to you, Colonel ben Levi. I'm glad to see you safely with us. Was it difficult to get the goods?'

Ari laughed easily, as if to dismiss any such preposterous assumptions. 'A piece of cake, Your Excellency, a real walkover. The extent to which you can rely on other people's stupidity and sloppiness to do your work has never ceased to amaze me.'

'Meaning?' asked Richard Armstrong.

'Meaning that due to the UN's financial crisis security has been significantly reduced, especially at night, which is when it happens to be especially necessary to prevent people like me from

324

getting up to mischief.' He smiled smugly. 'But that is not the way the cock-eyed UN Administration sees it. Anyhow, their total lack of foresight happens to have helped me no end in carrying this assignment out. It was a cinch to sneak out of the meeting of the Special Political Committee and find my way to Confidential Files.' He paused to light a cigarette, inhaled deeply and continued. 'As we had anticipated, Pulaski was working the night-shift alone. The rest, as I said, was a cinch. A needle-dart fired straight into the jugular and it was all over. The needle, gentlemen, carried a very special charge, Israel's best secret weapon to date. It is a substance, which for the moment shall remain nameless, and which our top scientists have developed to cause an ordinary heart attack. As Pulaski had a record of high blood pressure and circulatory trouble — despite which the inefficient UN Medical Service cleared him for a sensitive job — no one is going to think anything of his death, caused by a massive coronary. Because the man died of natural causes, no one is going to even imagine a file is missing from the archives,' he pointed to the briefcase on the table, 'much less that it is now in our possession. In there, gentlemen, you will find the confidential information you want on Kurt von Steuben.'

He picked up the bottle of Chivas Regal, poured himself a generous measure, and indicating the table with his glass, added graciously, 'Help yourselves. The information that file contains is enough to destroy von Steuben several times over. According to an independent panel of human rights experts, our current Secretary General appears to have had a somewhat murky record of collaboration with Nazi occupation forces in his beloved Austria at the time of the Anschluss which, according to his official biography, he staunchly opposed. The panel's version is somewhat different. Apparently, SS Lieutenant Kurt von Steuben was instrumental in the deportation of his Jewish countrymen, even showing zeal beyond the call of duty in rounding them up. The panel, you may be interested to know, was headed by Leo

Anders, then Professor of History at the University of Utrecht.'

'Then there was a connection . . . ' whispered Nikolai.

'Between the group's findings and Anders' death?' said Ari. 'Very probably, but it has to be proven. However, that will come later. First things first.'

'Why would von Steuben allow that file to remain in the archives?' wondered Armstrong.

'Who knows? He probably knew of an investigation that Anders, as Secretary General, intended to carry out, but he must have been totally unaware of the panel's earlier findings, and somehow certain that he had succeeded in erasing his past. The ancient Greeks had a word for that sort of smug pride — they called it *hubris*, and it was known to have caused the downfall of many a king. Well, the same sin will cause Mr von Steuben's downfall. In fact, it already has. He's yours, gentlemen.'

'At least for the moment,' smiled Nikolai Golovin. 'There is no greater hatred for the Nazis than in the Soviet

Union, except perhaps in Israel. Together with our American friends, we shall be able to control Mr von Steuben, and through him, policy in the United Nations Secretariat. Oh, not for any narrow selfish purposes, but because we believe we can improve the way it works.'

'Forgive me for being somewhat sceptical of that, Ambassador Golovin.' Colonel ben Levi looked at the Soviet diplomat with amusement.

'Please yourself, Colonel,' intervened Richard Armstrong. 'What my Soviet friend is saying is perfectly true — we want a better United Nations. But, with respect, I don't give a damn whether you Israelis believe us or not. What counts, as far as you are concerned, is that we will dangle this Damocles' sword over von Steuben's head throughout his five-year tenure, and then when he comes up for re-election, the United States and the Soviet Union will withdraw their support. At that time, we will hand him over to you. And now, gentlemen, I would like to propose a toast to our continuing co-operation.'

The three men raised their glasses in unison.

⋆   ⋆   ⋆

Galina let herself into her apartment, her right hand searching for the light switch on the wall. Before leaving for her evening meeting the night before, she had put the shutters down and the place was now in total darkness.

For the second time in less than twenty-four hours, utter shock paralyzed her completely.

Her flat had been ransacked.

Wherever she looked, there were clothes, books, papers strewn helter-skelter all over the floor. Her curtains had been ripped, as had her bed linen. Drawers were half pulled out and pictures wrenched off the walls. Whoever had broken in had left a vicious reminder of himself, for some warped reason she wholly failed to grasp.

In despair, she ran to her desk and rummaged in the second drawer, where she usually kept her important documents and the few valuables she possessed. Her hands madly sought the familiar bulk of a small embroidered silk purse where she had kept the few trinkets her mother had left her — a gold chain, a garnet bracelet, a coral and gold brooch. It was the brooch Galina especially treasured, because her mother had given it to her the year she died. It had been the last time she had a gift from a member of her family.

The purse was gone.

Helplessly, she sank to the floor as the room swam before her eyes, blind with uncontrollable tears. She wept for her lost mementos, but also for all her other bitter losses — for her family, for Nikolai, for her career, for all her smashed-up life.

Even as she sobbed, her grief was being edged out, replaced by a sudden terror that rose in her.

This was no ordinary robbery. It looked like just one of those almost routine New York break-ins, but it wasn't.

Someone must have seen her leaving

Pulaski's office, someone who was out to kill her.

Steady, Galina, she mumbled to herself, steady. Your friends have been robbed, so why not you? Just call the police and . . .

No. Not the police.

They'll arrest me and hand me over to *them*.

She had to get out of there, and fast. Run, run for her life before they came back and found her.

★   ★   ★

Galina raced up Third Avenue, wild-eyed, bumping into passers-by who turned to stare at the crazy girl wearing a thin dress in the dead of winter and fleeing from some unseen pursuer. Several times, she crossed the street, zigzagging between traffic that screeched to a halt among a volley of hooting and curses, then, unaccountably, crossed back again. At length, she was panting so heavily she was forced to slow her mad pace down to a fast walk. People gawked at her, even though New Yorkers are supposed to be inured to all manner of strangeness, but she did not care. All she needed was to reach some sort of haven, somewhere she could be safe from *them*.

She realized she had reached the upper Eighties, and an idea began to take shape in her mind. Surely he was the one person she could trust, surely he would not deny her sanctuary.

Five minutes later, she was ringing the bell of an apartment on Eighty-ninth and Third.

Dr Blum opened the door himself, still wearing his dressing-gown and slippers.

'Galina, what the hell . . . '

'Oh Dr Blum, please let me in, you've no idea what I've been through . . . Please . . . ' Again, she burst into a flood of tears.

'Yes, of course.' He stood back to let her pass, his eyes taking in her dishevelled hair, the staring eyes, the thin dress wet from the snow. 'What's the matter, child? You look as if you had run the New York marathon. And your clothes . . . Why, you'll catch pneumonia for certain,

running out like that in sub-zero temperatures . . . '

'Never mind the pneumonia, Dr Blum.'
She sank into an armchair in the living
room and closed her eyes wearily. 'I just
want someone to talk to . . . You knew my
parents, you know me, it's as if you were
family . . . ' Her voice trailed off.

'Of course, my dear, of course.' He sat
opposite her and took her cold hand in
his. 'What is it, child? You know you can
tell me everything . . . '

She sat bolt upright, and her feverish
eyes held the strangest glimmer he had
ever seen. 'Well, I know it sounds crazy,
but . . . ' she glanced over her shoulder
and her voice dropped to a barely audible
whisper. 'Dr Blum, I have reason to
suspect that Secretary General Anders
was assassinated and that there is a
conspiracy at the United Nations, a
conspiracy of such proportions that . . . '

★ ★ ★

Dr Blum paced the floor of his surgery
like a caged animal, an anxious frown on

his face. He turned to his wife, who looked back at him and shook her head sadly. She, too, was bitterly sorry for Galina, who was almost like a daughter to her.

'Bella,' sighed the doctor, 'don't you see that, as a physician, I have no choice? Galina is a very, very sick girl and she badly needs help. If I let her go, she's likely to harm herself, to . . . '

'Leonard, you can't just have the girl locked up, maybe put away for years because she happens to be a bit overwrought. Where is she now, anyway?'

'In the bedroom, asleep. I persuaded her to take a sedative which will give her a chance to rest. Meantime, I'll make the necessary arrangements.'

'You mean . . . '

'Precisely. I'm phoning Dr Nussbaum, the Director of Psychiatry at Manhattan General to arrange for Galina's immediate admission.'

'Because she happens to be depressed. She hasn't had it easy, you know . . . '

'I know, and maybe that's why she's totally lost her grip on reality. You've no idea how she rants and raves about some conspiracy at the United Nations and the Secretary General's murder. You know, it hurts me terribly to see her like that and the sooner she gets help, the better it will be for her.'

★ ★ ★

She seemed to be emerging from centuries of sleep, and at first she could not focus on the room. There seemed to be people, voices. Where was she? Painfully, she opened her eyes and Dr Blum's kind, concerned face floated into her line of vision. Behind him, she could see two men in white.

Instead of the dress she had been wearing when she went to sleep in Dr Blum's apartment, what she had on was some kind of shapeless, coarsely sewn garment that felt rough and unpleasant on her skin. Even the bed felt different, hard and without any pillows to rest her head on. Slowly, she raised her eyes and saw that the windows were barred.

The full horror of the situation dawned

335

on her. She had trusted Dr Blum enough to share her terrible secret with him, and he had betrayed her.

'You bastard!' she yelled, 'you slimy double-crossing bastard! I'll kill you, you unspeakable scum!' She tried to jump up, but the men in white rushed forward and pinned her to the bed.

She felt the sharp stab of a needle in her arm, then nothing.

New York, April 1987

'You see, unfortunately Miss Romanova is not showing any improvement. She has not responded to drugs or therapy, and has instead lapsed into a totally catatonic state punctuated by bouts of schizophrenic delusions,' Dr Nussbaum recited in a flat monotone. 'So before taking the decision to commit her permanently, my colleagues Dr Chen and Dr Walton and I feel it's only appropriate to talk to all those who know her. You see, she has no family to contest the decision of three qualified psychiatrists to commit her to a psychiatric institution. Once we sign, as required by law, only three of our colleagues can revoke the ruling.'

The man who sat facing the three doctors nodded respectfully.

'It's only proper, then,' continued Dr Nussbaum, 'that we seek the opinion of the girl's former employers. Tell me, Mr Crimer, in your opinion, was Galina Romanova unbalanced?'

Basil Crimer looked suitably sombre. 'Unfortunately, Dr Nussbaum,' he sighed heavily, 'I can only confirm your diagnosis. You see, when I first met her two years ago at the Geneva summit, she seemed . . . well, normal, sort of, though a bit high-strung. When I joined the United Nations as Head of the Conference Division, it was brought to my attention that her behaviour was becoming increasingly erratic and that it was beginning to affect her work in the booth.'

'In your opinion, do you think any of her colleagues could add anything to what you have told us?'

'I doubt it. They would probably

confirm what I have said.' And God help those who don't, he added to himself.

'Thank you very much, Mr Crimer.'

'Thank you, gentlemen.'

★ ★ ★

'Well, you've now heard Dr Blum, Miss Romanova's personal physician, as well as her supervisor at work, not to mention Mr William Hewitt, her former fiancé, who agrees that her behaviour in the last few months has been very strange indeed.' He peered at his two colleagues, who sat impassively listening to him, not registering any human emotion whatsoever. 'It is my considered opinion,' he concluded, 'that Miss Galina Romanova is a chronic paranoid schizophrenic and that she is incurable. She is therefore to be immediately committed to New York State Psychiatric Hospital for further treatment. Dr Chen?' The Chinese psychiatrist nodded repeatedly. 'Dr Walton?'

Dr Alvin Walton, the grey eminence of American psychiatric medicine, sat stock-still for a few minutes, staring absently into space. 'Dr Walton?' Dr Nussbaum was getting impatient. The Romanova case had already given him no end of trouble, what with her wall of silence broken by savage outbursts and volleys of insults directed at him and his colleagues. He would be glad to be rid of her, palming her off on to the staff at the New York State facility.

'Dr Walton?' he repeated with some irritation.

'I'll sign,' Alvin Walton said quietly.

The three men appended their signatures certifying that Galina Romanova was incurably insane and referring her to New York State Psychiatric Hospital for the remainder of her days.

Epilogue

'Miss Romanova, you have a visitor. Miss Romanova?'

The nurse shook her head sadly and glanced at the tall, distinguished man who stood next to her. 'I'm afraid you won't get much of a response from this patient, sir. Since she came to us from Manhattan General eight years ago, she has become more and more withdrawn until she stopped talking altogether. Even the doctors have given up on her. She just sits there, oblivious to her surroundings. Such a sad, sad case. Are you a friend of hers, then? I believe she has no relatives.'

'Yes, a very old friend.'

'Well, good luck then, but I don't think she'll recognize you.'

He could hardly believe what he saw. The pretty, lively girl he had known over ten years ago was now a fat, shapeless old woman with pale sunken eyes and hollow cheeks. Her skin was yellowish and blotchy and she sat hunched on her bed, her mouth slightly open and dribbling like a baby.

He approached her gently, as if not to frighten her, and sat down opposite her, taking both her hands in his and looking into her vacant eyes. 'Galina,' he said softly, 'Galya. *Pomnish menya?*'

She looked at him with empty eyes.

'Do you remember me?' he repeated.

Still she stared into the distance.

Nikolai turned away, unable to cope with the horror he was witnessing. He knew now he should never have come, but when his former colleague Alexei Filatov told him that Galina Romanova was confined to a psychiatric institution, he felt he somehow owed it to her to see her again. He had never been able to find out what had happened, for no one seemed to know, and his position as Soviet Ambassador to the United Nations precluded him from getting too involved with the staff. No one knew he was here, and, as far as he was concerned, no one ever would, least of all his wife Natalia.

He tightened his hold on her limp

hands. *Dorogaya* Galina, he thought, if you only knew what happened after you left the world of the living, if you had been able to see the tinder-box going up in flames, nearly destroyed by the biggest scandal in its history . . .

My dear Galina, how you would have laughed if only you had seen the amazement on von Steuben's face when he learnt that the United States and the Soviet Union would not support his re-election as Secretary General. That was, as I recall, back in 1991. If you had only been able to enjoy the massive news coverage of von Steuben's extradition hearings and his being handed over to Israeli authorities to be tried for Nazi war crimes. And if you could have only seen his snivelling plea for mercy just before his execution by hanging in Tel Aviv back in June, 1992 . . .

Do you know, Galina, that von Steuben's last few days on Death Row were not free of their sordid aspect, either, when he learned that his helpmate, his beloved Anneliese, had left for South America with Basil Crimer, where they settled under assumed names and lived for many years following the former Secretary General's execution. To this day, the happy couple are believed to be somewhere in Argentina or Brazil, though no one really knows . . .

For a brief moment, he thought he saw a glimmer of lucidity pass through her eyes and, full of hope, he looked at her more closely. No, there was nothing there. He must have imagined it.

He let go of her hands and turned away and hastily left the room without looking back at her.

As he drove back to Manhattan in the gentle spring twilight, a nagging question tugged at the back of his mind, a question only Galina herself could ever have answered.

He wondered who or what was responsible for Galina's rapid and relentless descent into madness. When he knew her briefly in Geneva all those years ago, she had seemed totally balanced and sound of mind. Shortly thereafter, according to Alexei Filatov and other colleagues, she was an inmate in Manhattan General, then transferred to a New York State hospital for the incurably insane. He wondered if she, as Leo Anders, had been silenced because she knew too much.

He had been so lost in thought that he had not realized where he was until a familiar building loomed ahead of him. With the setting sun reflecting off its myriad windows, the United Nations Secretariat building appeared to be aflame.

The tinder-box was burning.